# Gone to Blazes

In the Longhorn saloon in the rambunctious gold rush town of White Oaks, New Mexico, the beautiful Selina dances seductively for the miners. And it's love at first sight for the naive young sawyer, Vince. He's no fast gun, so what chance has he when Texan killer Cotton Bulloch muscles in on the saloon profits, kidnaps and rapes Selina and forces her to be his girl?

Meanwhile, the area is being flooded with forged greenbacks by a gang led by shady Jake Blackman. Can Sheriff Pat Garrett arrest both Bulloch and Blackman and his boys? Or, as the Longhorn erupts in a hail of bullets must Vince face the murderous Texan in single combat? Can his love for Selina be doomed?

*By the same author*

# Gone to Blazes

Jackson Davis

**A Black Horse Western**

ROBERT HALE · LONDON

© Jackson Davis 2011
First published in Great Britain 2012

ISBN 978-0-7090-9351-0

Robert Hale Limited
Clerkenwell House
Clerkenwell Green
London EC1R 0HT

www.halebooks.com

The right of Jackson Davis to be identified as
author of this work has been asserted by him
in accordance with the Copyright, Designs and
Patents Act 1988

Typeset by
Derek Doyle & Associates, Shaw Heath
Printed and bound in Great Britain by
CPI Antony Rowe, Chippenham and Eastbourne

# ONE

The lithe and sinuous dark-haired girl danced as if possessed, her loose skirt whirling to reveal bronzed thighs, her slim arms held high, bare feet twirling on the table top as Spanish guitars strummed, fiddles screeched and an Indian drum reverberated to the fast staccato rythym.

The Longhorn saloon was jam packed; a bunch of miners and travellers, who had hoisted the girl on to the table, roared their lusty and lustful appreciation, stomping their boots and clapping their horny hands, urging her on.

Selina Shawcross's entangled curls looked like a knot of writhing black snakes as she madly tossed them about, her eyes flashing, her well-formed breasts bouncing, half-exposed by the loose-cut scarlet blouse.

'Selina!' Aaron Shawcross had shouldered his way through the excited throng to stand before her. Pointing an accusing finger, he shouted at the top of his lungpower, 'Cease! Get down from there.'

Th half-Mexican girl froze as she met his eyes, then bowed low, giving the men an even better opportunity to view her assets. 'Aw, let her be,' a miner yelled, amid hisses and catcalls. 'She was just gittin' goin'.'

Selina held her pose for a few seconds, then skipped down to join her father. He grabbed her by her blouse and shook her hard. 'Look at you, showing off your body. Aren't you ashamed?'

'Aw, Pa, I didn't mean no harm. They asked me to dance. What's wrong in dancing?'

'You call that dancing?' He dragged her away to the back of the saloon. 'It's as if you've got the devil inside you. Don't you see how you inflame their lusts? No good can come of it. Why don't you behave like a decent young lady?'

'Aw.' Selina scraped her hair back and pouted her full rosy lips. 'I cain't help wanting to dance. It don't mean I'm bad, Pa.'

Aaron Shawcross relented and smiled sadly at his daughter. He was attired in the manner of a Southern gentleman, which was what he had once been, slave-holder and master of a Kentucky mansion, until the war destroyed all that.

On his own, he had crossed the great Mississippi and wandered haphazardly for years through the south-west. He had married a Mexican woman and found happiness for a while. She had died of the fever when Selina was six years old. So he and his daughter had wandered on together. But fortune had always eluded Aaron.

His once black, velvet-collared frock-coat had the zinc-green sheen of age, his shirt cuffs were frayed, his silk waistcoat stained, his boots coming apart at the seams, his wide-brimmed hat was greasy and past its better days. He affected the airs and graces of a Southern gentleman, which made him something of a laughing stock. And he plied the profession of a gambling man. What else could he do? Playing cards was his only skill.

'You sit here, dear, and behave yourself.' Aaron patted her hair into place. 'I must try my luck in the poker game. Our funds are very low. Remember, have nothing to do with any of these men. Most are scoundrels and cut-throats and after only one thing.'

'What's that, Pa?' Selina asked, her blue eyes twinkling mischievously.

'To ruin you, that's what. You must beware. Perhaps you had better go back to our room now. I could be here 'til the early hours.'

'Just let me stay an hour or so, Pa. I promise I'll be good. I like listening to the music.'

The Mexican musicians on the podium were strumming and crooning to a more plangent, sentimental number. 'Very well,' Aaron agreed. 'Just an hour. Then you go straight home and lock the door until I get back.'

'Good luck, Pa,' Selina called, as he headed away through the crowded tables, past the spinning Wheel of Fortune and the sign of the Bengal Tiger above the faro table. The air was thick with smoke from tobacco and the flicker of oil lamps and soon he was lost in the hubbub of men and voices.

They had drifted south this past summer, leaving Santa Fe and Las Vegas and travelled by stagecoach deep into the wilder parts of New Mexico, passing through Fort Sumner, where the notorious outlaw, Billy the Kid, had recently been gunned down. Then they followed the Pecos grasslands, branched off up the Hondo and the Rio Bonito to Lincoln, and on through the mountains to this gold-rich town of White Oaks.

'Here,' Aaron Shawcross had vowed, 'our luck will change.'

How right he was, but it was not to be in the way he expected.

'Hi!' A curly-haired youth had slipped into the other chair at the table. 'Mind if I jine ya?'

Remembering her father's admonitions Selina primly pursed her lips and shrugged. 'It's a free country.'

'Yeah. I watched you dancing. Wow! You were a knock-out.'

'Really?' The girl could not restrain a smile. 'You think so?'

'Yeah, are you a professional? I mean, do they pay you? I mean, do you work here?'

'Certainly not.' She scowled and looked away. 'I ain't a cathouse gal. So don't you go thinkin' I am.'

'Sorry, sweetheart, I didn't mean to imply. . . .' The youth blushed with confusion beneath his suntan. 'I meant just a dancer. I mean, you're great.'

'I ain't your sweetheart, neither. So don't you go callin' me that. My name's Selina Shawcross and my daddy's a gentleman of the gambling fraternity. That's why I come here, so there. Now you know.'

'Sure, miss . . . uh . . . um . . . Selina, don't git het up.' He could have been a cowhand from one of the ranches, dressed as he was in worn blue denims held up by a bit of cord pulled tight around his slim waist, a black velvet shirt and a straw sunhat, but there were no spurs on his boots and no revolver on view. 'Just thought I'd say hello. My name's Vince. How about I buy you a drink?'

'Oh, no. I don't drink. I'm only fifteen.'

'Try one of them canned tomato juices. They're OK.' Before she could refuse he had ordered from a passing waiter. 'You must need something after all that dancin'.'

'Why, thank you.' She swept a catlike glance at him. 'You ain't a cowboy, and you're certainly not a miner. What is it you do?'

'I work over at Blazer's Mills, not so far from here. The sawmill and grist mill. Hard work, but it's OK. Gets a bit boring, same thang every day. That's why I hit out for here. It's real exciting, all these different folks and bright lights. Then I got to see you. That was best of all.'

'Well.' She frowned. 'Don't get too excited.

9

Remember what I told you. I gotta be goin' home soon, anyhow.'

Vince grinned at her as the drinks arrived. He clinked his beer to her glass. 'This is what I really call living.'

Sweat pricked from the brow of Aaron Shawcross as he watched the play of the cards, a sweat either of anger or of righteous indignation. He had been sure he had held, on several occasions, the winning combination, but each time his adversary beat him. He knew he was being cheated but he couldn't tell how.

Inexorably, fifty of his dollars had been whittled away, dollars he could ill afford to lose. Now, as he dug into his coat pocket for his last few coins he tried not to show his alarm. Pale of complexion from days and nights spent in gambling dens, and languid of manner, his blue, innocent-looking eyes assessed the lanky Jake Blackman seated opposite him.

'Are you in or out, mister?' Blackman's own dark eyes flickered with amused contempt, his wolfish jaws seeming to drool as he eyed the prospect of raking in the pot. 'If you're in you better come up with more cash.'

'This is all I have.' Shawcross affected an uncaring disdain as he tossed the silver across. But he was smouldering with anger inside. 'You may as well rook me for all I've got.'

Maybe his luck would change. Maybe he could win on the last throw. The misguided hope of how many millions of addicted gamblers throughout time? But hope, nonetheless.

Aaron Shawcross was certainly a different kettle of fish from the Pikey. A native of Pike County, Missouri, Blackman was one of the worst of his breed, shifty, low-minded, and always ready to do a man down. He had marked Aaron out as a dreamer, ready for the plucking.

'Sure, you tailor's dummy, count your cards.' Jake was roughly garbed in a coat cut, surely, by a hacksaw, heavy boots, trousers like concertinas held up by a thick belt into which was shoved a a long-barrelled Buntline Special. His dark jackdaw eyes gleamed from beneath the brim of a floppy black hat and met those of a slatternly saloon waitress, as Aaron pre-pared to make his play. She was standing behind the Kentuckian, a tray of beers on her arm, watching his choice of cards. She touched her ear and scratched below her breast five times. Blackman understood the prearranged signal and his grin widened.

'Bring me one of them beers, Nell,' he called.

She came around and placed the tray on the table beside him, pouring from a jug into a tumbler. Under cover of her bulk Jake deftly removed the ace of hearts she held beneath the tray, and relinquished a card he did not need.

Shawcross looked up from his cards and spotted them. 'Wait a minute. What's going on?'

'Whadda ya mean,' Blackman growled. 'She's just pouring me a beer. You want one? If not, play your

11

hand, mister.'

Shawcross watched him, his blue eyes alert. Yes, something had passed hands between the woman and the Pikey, of that he was sure. But what? This time he had a good hand. He couldn't be beaten, surely? 'I'll go for it,' he said, and spread his cards. 'The whole pot.'

'Too bad, pal,' Jake Blackman drawled. 'I jest happen to have an ace in the hole.'

Shawcross stared at the ace in the Pikey's winning hand, watched him start to draw in the pile of dollars, saw all he possessed, his dreams of a better life, going, going, gone. In spite of the fear in him of Blackman and his cronies seated around the table in the crowded saloon, he blurted out his accusations. 'Where did you get that ace from? Give me my money back, you lousy cheat. I know what's been going on.'

'You what?' Jake Blackman froze in the act of stuffing the cash into his pockets. 'What did you call me?'

'I said you're a filthy, stinking cheat. You just leave that cash where it is. I've had enough of this. That woman is in on it.'

'Me?' Nell screamed. 'What the hell you talkin' about?'

'*You* know what,' Shawcross answered. 'You've been passing him cards. Where else did he get that ace from?'

'You better be prepared to back those words, mister?'

Aaron Shawcross heard the growling threat in

Blackman's words, saw his hand slide across to the butt of his revolver. In a flash of a second he knew his choice. He could swallow his words, eat humble pie, get up and walk out of there with their laughter ringing in his ears. Or he could fight.

He chose, foolishly, to fight.

From his coat pocket Aaron pulled a small two-shot derringer, cocked the hammer, and aimed it at Blackman. At the same instant there was the flash and crash of an explosion, a thud in his chest that sent him hurtling back: he felt an excruciating pain, a giddiness and weakness, and he heard his derringer clatter to the floor as he slowly slid down the wall and lay beside it. He put a hand to his heart and stared at the blood ebbing through his fingers, at first with disbelief, and then with the sickening realization that it was his lifeblood and he was done for. 'Tell Selina,' he groaned, 'I'm sorry. . . .'

Jake Blackman watched the life flow out of the man on the floor and refrained from wasting another bullet on him. 'He's a goner,' he said coldly, as he scooped up the rest of the cash. 'Some men cain't bear to be losers. Y'all saw him. He pulled his l'il gun on me. What was I s'posed to do?'

'You did right,' Nell stoutly agreed, her arms akimbo. 'He'd got no right saying that about you, Jake. And fancy saying that to me? The cheek.'

'No man says that to me and gets away with it,' Blackman growled, as he pushed a few dollars over to her.

13

'That's for your trouble, Nell.'

The shabby men in the saloon stared at Blackman as he shoved through them, the 16-inch-barrelled revolver hanging loosely from his hand. They watched as he pushed through the batwing doors, climbed on to his horse and ambled it away up the muddy main street. They returned their gaze to the corpse of the gambler.

'Somebody better go tell his daughter,' someone said.

# TWO

Cotton Bulloch spurred his mustang up an arroyo, his nostrils twitching as he smelled fire. But there was no sign of smoke. A cautious, some said a crazy and crafty man, he pulled his Remington from his holster and clicked the cylinder on to a live round. When he reached the crest of the hill he saw a small creek running down towards the bank of the Rio Hondo. He made out the remains of a fire beside the stream. There was a cookpan balanced on stones above the smouldering ashes. It was as if somebody had been in the process of cooking a meal. And then he saw the 'somebody' lying face down in the water.

'Hello!' he called, sharply at first, thinking the man might be drinking from the stream. But there was a fixity about the body that spoke of death. Then he saw the blood curdling away in the current. Bulloch glanced around. There was no sign of life on the bleak mountainsides. The only sound was that of the constant wind. So he stepped down, reached for

15

the man's besuited shoulder and hauled him back over, face up. A gaping wound in the throat made even Bulloch wince, and he'd seen plenty of death in his time.

'Looks like they got his jugular. One clean slash,' he muttered. 'Musta bled like a pig as he tumbled into the stream.'

Most of the blood had gone now and in its rictus of death the face of the corpse already had a grey pallor. Whoever he was, he must have been a man of some substance, Cotton Bulloch surmised, because his well-tailored, three-piece suit was of top grade tweed in a dark-chocolate herringbone pattern, his blood-red boots were well-tooled, and he wore a gold ring on one finger. A loose, spotted bandanna, hitched at the back of the neck to serve as a dust-mask, had kept his blue shirt relatively unstained. His trouser pockets were empty, fore and aft, pulled out as if he had been hastily searched. The same went for the pockets of his jacket and vest. If he had been wearing a body belt that, too, had been stolen.

Who was this jasper? Bulloch wondered.

The dead man was in his early thirties, not unhandsome in a hirsute way when he had been alive, clean-shaven apart from his heavy moustache, which was neatly trimmed like his dark hair. Bulloch pulled off one of his boots and found the maker's mark: Santa Fe. The capital of New Mexico was many miles north of here.

In the dust, carelessly tossed away after being

looted of its cash, was a leather wallet. It was empty but for a shiny metal federal marshal's badge tucked into one side, beneath which was a card giving his name as William Dunwoody, officer of the law, with authority to arrest and transport felons cross-border for crimes against the federal laws.

'Whoo!' Bulloch gave a whistle of awe and scratched at the month-long growth of beard about his own jaw. 'Who'd a' guessed this snitch was in the vicinity?'

Cotton Bulloch had for long had an inbred hatred of law-enforcers, or for that matter anybody in authority. Then another thought occurred. 'Hey, he might well a' been after me, only a jump ahead. Whoever done this maybe done me a favour.'

This southern part of New Mexico was a wild, sparsely populated part of the world. Travellers on the trail were few and far between apart from the twice-weekly stage. Then he remembered the two evil-looking Mexicans he had encountered on the trail, riding two up on a sturdy Morgan stallion. That itself was suspicious and Bulloch had drawn his Remington and kept it trained on them as they approached.

'Aiee, *hombre*, why you so unfriendly?' one had yelled, grinning gold-glinting teeth. 'You got whiskey to sell? Don' worry, we rich, we pay you.'

'Get lost,' Bulloch had growled, and spurred his mustang past them as their shrill cackling blew away on the wind.

17

Now another idea hit him as he jigged the wallet up and down in his palm. The 'fed' was of the same muscular build, not unsimilar in appearance to himself. Bulloch pulled a Wanted bill – or small poster – from his own back pocket.

Beneath a poor daguerrotype likeness of himself were the words:

> Cotton Bulloch, aged 33 years, dark hair, brown eyes, medium height, 5ft 9ins., strong build, wanted for rape, arson, bank robbery, kidnap, torture and homicide.
>
> Fort Worth authorities will pay a reward of $1,000 for his capture dead or alive.

'Yeah,' Bulloch grinned sardonically. He caught hold of his mustang's reins and let it drink from the stream, then loosened the saddle cinch and ground-hitched the horse. 'Maybe they will.'

He found some dry kindling amid a clump of pines, fanned the ashes and soon had the jasper's coffee pot bubbling. He pulled off his own filthy, sweat-stained shirt, his battered boots, his worn blue jeans and holey, faded long johns until he stood in the hot sun stark naked apart from his greasy Stetson, and sipped at a tin mug of the scalding black brew. He put it aside and stripped the lawman. 'Hmm, just my fit,' he said, as he pulled on the blue shirt, the dark-brown suit, and the new boots, which were a bit too large but better than being too small.

It was difficult with a dead weight, but he managed to dress the man in his own discarded dirty old clothes, swapped hats, stuffing his own Stetson in a pocket of the tattered macinaw he pushed the stiff's arms into. Luckily, full rigor mortis had not yet set in.

'I'll have this,' he muttered, buckling on the jasper's empty gunbelt. Any weapon and bullets on it had disappeared, along with the man's cash. He stuck his own Remington into the holster for the time being. 'Right!' He opened his arms to the mustang. 'Behold, the new man. How do I look?' The horse gazed at him and blew a raspberry, shaking its mane.

'Aw, whadda *you* know, you dumb brute.' Bulloch trussed the 'fed' with his lariat, winding it around the man's ankles and hitching the rawhide rope to his saddle horn. He swung on to the saddle. 'C'mon, you lazy varmint, let's git.'

The reason his old clothes looked so travel-worn was that he had come a long distance in the past month, leaving all that horror behind him in Fort Worth, travelling alone across Texas, going on and on, risking losing his scalp as he headed west through the eroded, rutted Staked Plains, a region still infested with wandering Comanches. He had reached, at last, the ranch lands of New Mexico, the Pecos cow country where, after the recent internecine range wars, Chisum still reigned supreme. His star shootist, Billy 'the Kid' Bonney, had been gunned down at the age of twenty-one, which maybe wasn't a a bad thing.

And so Cotton Bulloch had gone on, up the Rio Hondo tributary, heading for Lincoln, following the winding stagecoach trail, putting Texas far behind him.

Earlier that day he had cast off on a narrow pony trail through high rocks that looked as if it might be a short cut, unsuitable for a coach, following the river. It seemed the lawman had had the same idea, pausing there to cook up his breakfast. And there he had met the Mexicans and his fate. Now he was bumping along in the dust behind Bulloch, who was intent on rejoining the trail up into the mountains.

'With luck we'll be in Lincoln by sundown,' Cotton Bulloch gritted out as he spat in the dust and raked the mustang's sides, urging it onward.

Sheriff Pat Garrett was sitting on the high veranda above the porticoed entrance to Lincoln County Court House, taking his first bite of the bottle that evening, when he saw the stranger ride in with what looked like a corpse bumping along in the dust behind him.

'Hey, mister,' he called, getting to his feet. 'Who in holy tarnation's the stiffie?'

'Seems like he's wanted in Texas so I've brought him in.' Cotton eased his bronco and peered up. 'Where's the sheriff of this town?'

'I *am* the sheriff. Wait there. I'll be down.' Garrett laid his whiskey aside and clambered down a steep stairway to the dusty road. In his tall Stetson and high-heeled boots he towered over Cotton, who had dismounted. In a five-button suit Garrett was as immaculately rigged out as the stranger. 'Nope.' He shook his head. 'Cain't say I recognize him.'

Cotton breathed an inward sigh of relief at the news. 'I found him with his throat cut, off the trail, back about ten miles. It's my guess he was bush-whacked at his camp by a couple of greasers I met earlier on. They were two up on a Morgan stallion and it sure didn't look like theirs.'

'You saying you didn't kill him?'

'Nope, I didn't kill him. He'd been robbed. All he had on him was this.' Cotton handed over his Wanted notice.

'Cotton Bulloch,' the sheriff muttered. 'Never heard of him. But it seems, like you say, he's on the lam.'

'Yeah, from the look of his clothes he's had a long, hard ride.'

'So?' Garrett turned a gimlet grey eye on the swarthy stranger. 'Who the hell are you?'

Cotton showed him the wallet. 'Marshal Will Dunwoody, as you see.'

'Yeah?' Garrett grinned a mouthful of horsey teeth. 'Got a message from Santa Fe to say you were on your way. So, dump that character in the shade, see to your hoss and come upstairs.'

Garrett was perusing the poster again when Cotton joined him. He brandished it at him. 'A thousand reward. A pity you cain't collect.'

'I can't?' This was news to Bulloch, who picked up the proferred glass of cowherder's delight and took a gulp. 'Salud!'

'Don't put that act on. You well know a federal marshal ain't entitled to any state rewards. On the other hand county sheriff could claim.'

'You could,' Cotton somewhat doubtfully agreed. 'But on the other hand you didn't find him, so you ain't entitled, if you don't mind me saying so, Sheriff.'

'Feel free to speak your mind, Marshal. But I guess, on the piss-all pay and expenses you make, you wouldn't turn your nose up at five hundred?'

'You mean, you'll claim you caught him and we'll go halves?'

'Sure; you're gonna be in the vicinity for a while sniffin' out these forgers. I'm sorry to say I ain't got no leads, except fake greenbacks, not exactly good quality, seem to be emanating from the town of White Oaks up the valley another forty-five miles. I wish you luck, my friend.'

'Yeah.' Cotton eased his back in a basket chair beside the sheriff and savoured the whiskey. 'So, I'm on my own on this?'

'I'm a busy man, Will. Got a lot on my plate. And it looks like I'd better be after those two Mexicans. I like the sound of that Morgan horse. Just the breed I could do with. Must be worth a coupla hundred, at least.'

'Them murderin' varmints might well have some stolen cash on them, too.'

Garrett grinned again. 'Yes, that had crossed my mind.'

'Another perk of your trade?'

'Aw, no, marshal, you know I'd hand it in, if they ain't already spent it all, of course.'

'Of course.'

'You see this veranda? The very one Billy the Kid harangued the townsfolk from after he blasted Deputies Bob Olinger and Jim Bell to Kingdom Come when he busted outa jail.'

'Yeah? You don't say. I understand it was you, Sheriff, who finally gunned him down.'

'True, Marshal. You've probably read some of the snidey stories in the press about me waiting for him in a darkened room at Fort Sumner, not giving the little angel a chance to defend hisself. That boy was only twenty-one but had killed twenty-one men, including Sheriff Brady right over there in the middle of the street. He was a cold-blooded killer. What chance would *you* have given him?'

'None at all. It was him or you, Sheriff. You did the right thing.'

'Yeah, we can't follow the rules all the time. All that crap about calling out to 'em to identify 'emselves and surrender.'

'I ain't got no time for that, neither.'

'All those dime novels about him are to blame. Folks seem to think Billy was the hero and me the villain. Just how stupid can they be?'

'True, Sheriff.'

There was a bitter twist to Garrett's lips beneath the heavy moustache as he finished his drink. 'I got political ambitions, so I could do with some *good* publicity. I ain't planning on being a county sheriff the rest of my days. Come on, let's go eat.'

'Yeah, great. I'm starvin'.'

As the two men got to their feet, Garrett patted Cotton on the shoulder and drawled, 'By the way, there's about four hundred folks live in and around this li'l town of ourn and most of 'em, including my wife, are Latino. So we don't really favour the term greaser.'

'Right, Pat, I'll bear that in mind,' Cotton muttered. 'It's just that these two gold-teeth-grinning jackanapes just looked like typical ... er ... Mexicans.'

# THREE

The rain lashed down as Selina Shawcross watched the rough pine coffin being lowered into the hole in the ground.

'We bring nothing into this world and 'tis to be sure we take nothing out,' the preacher intoned.

He was a Unitarian and she had been lucky to get his services for a small fee, for she and her father had not been members of his congregation.

She clutched her shawl around her, trying to hear his words as the undertaker and his assistant began hurriedly to fill in the hole and her father disappeared from her life for ever.

'Bid his soul *adieu*,' the preacher cried, as she stared at the rough-hewn grave marker that she and Vincent had hammered into the ground. On the wood she had burned with a hot poker the words, 'Aaron Shawcross, 1842-83, killed by black-harted card cheet.'

She had wanted to name Jake Blackman, but

Vince had persuaded her that wasn't a good idea. 'Cain't you kill him for me?' she had cried, for the youth was with her in the room when they brought the news.

'Selina, all I got is a shotgun,' he had protested. 'I'm pretty good at pottin' rats around the barn, rabbits, or foxes and coyotes when they raid the 'coop, but I ain't no gunman. I wouldn't stand a chance aginst Blackman and his gang.'

Vince's curls were plastered down by the rain as he hung on to her arm and he heard her hiss, 'Father will be avenged. If *you* won't do it, I'll do it myself, or find somebody who will.'

The preacher, in his black suit and hat, looked like a bedraggled crow as he called out, 'Friends, let us join in that grand old hymn, "To the Sweet Beyond",' and the handful of mourners hesitantly and croakily began to sing.

Selina leaned forward as if she would throw herself sobbing upon the grave as the earth was pounded down. It was the last she would ever see of the noble, dreamy, learned man who had given her life, raised her, protected her, tried to teach her to do right. 'All over a few dollars,' she whispered, as Vincent hung on to her. 'What a waste.'

The mourners were hurrying off through the rain back to the town. 'What are ye going to do now, girl?' the preacher demanded. 'Fifteen is terrible young to lose a father.'

Selina knew only a terrible lostness and aloneness.

26

Perhaps her tears were partly out of self-pity. 'I dunno,' she said. 'I dunno what I'll do. I guess I'll get by.'

The preacher clutched his big Bible to his chest. 'Be careful whom you take up with, girl. Avoid all Mormons like the plague. Stay clear of Missourans. Like Jake Blackman they are shiftless rogues with evil in their hearts.'

'What does Blackman *do*?' Vince put in.

The preacher gave the youth a withering regard. 'He claims to be a cattle drover. For the moment I believe he hangs out at some run-down hide-out in the hills. But he's one who never settles to any good. The cattle are generally other people's, which he's purloined. He's just a murdering drunkard, thief and blackguard. And he's not the only one in these parts with those sad qualities.'

'So he just shoots my father, takes the cash, walks out of the saloon and nobody tries to stop him?'

'As I understand it both men drew on each other. By the so-called Law of the West it was a fair fight. It happens too frequently in these parts.'

Selina shivered as she pulled the sodden shawl around her. 'Pa was like that. If he thought he was wronged he said so.'

' 'Tis not the wisest thing to call a man a cheat when that man's Jake Blackman, he has a gun in his hand and the devil in his heart.'

'Pa once owned a big plantation. He was clever. He taught me to read and write. But I guess he was a fool, too, to get hisself kilt over a pot of a few dollars.'

'A pretty lass like you.' The preacher took in her slender form, the ripe fullness of her breasts, the nipples protuberant through the sodden dress which was plastered to her by now. 'An innocent abroad among the wolves. I don't envy your chances, girl. Come to think of it, out of Christian charity I might find you a place as a help in my household.'

Selina knew the preacher lived in a wooden-frame house, with a somewhat dowdy wife. 'Father allus said Unitarians had sensible beliefs,' she replied thoughtfully.

'Indeed, we have.' The preacher put a 'fatherly' arm around her, gave her a squeeze and put his mouth close to her ear. 'He was right there. You would not have many chores to do, girl, if you pleased me.'

'No, I'd rather not.' Selina shied away from him. Too many men had tried to paw her and look at her like that. 'Vince says he will try to help me.'

'Pah, he's just a boy. What can he offer you?'

Selina stepped away and for the first time that day scornfully smiled. 'Anyway, I'd rather stay free for a while.'

'Hah! Heed my warning, girl,' the preacher shouted. 'Or the devil will surely get you. *Acutus decensus Avernii.* Steep is the slide into Hell.'

'Yes, I will heed you,' she cried, turning on her heel. 'I ain't no sinner. I don't want no man touching me.'

It had been late at night when they brought her the news of her father's death. They had been chatting on the porch beneath the stars. But Selina had got into such a state at the news that Vince decided to stay to give his support. She had let him into the room and collapsed on her bed. Vince had kneeled beside the girl, patting her shoulder, comforting her, stroking her hair. In fact, an insidious urge had possessed him to slip in beside her . . . but how could he do that, take advantage of her, on such a night?

When she had at last fallen asleep he rested on her father's bunk. He should have been getting back to the mill. It was a long ride of about forty miles across the backhills. But it was Sunday, so he had stayed, helped her find the preacher, arrange the burial.

By now it was getting late in the afternoon. 'You ought to put on some dry clothes,' he advised, after they had trudged back to her room through the rain.

'You turn your back while I do,' she said, so he busied himself lighting the stove to dry his shirt and her frock and shawl. 'Why don't you take off your pants,' she suggested. 'Dry them off, too.'

'Aw, no, they're all right.'

'You're sweet, Vince.' Salina smiled. 'No need to be shy of me. I know I can trust you.'

Yes, he thought, but could he trust himself?

Selina began looking through her father's possessions, what few there were. 'Look!' She took a converted Navy revolver from his small trunk. 'He had this in the cavalry in the war. A pity he didn't have it with him last night. He might have taught that Jake Blackman a good lesson.'

And then she found, beneath a shirt, a twenty-dollar gold piece. She held it aloft. 'Look, he had this all the time. Come on, Vince. Let's go eat. I need to change this cartwheel into smaller coins.'

It was good to see her looking more cheerful. Vince treated her, and himself, to a couple of drinks in the saloon. Up at the bar getting served he looked back and saw the slatternly waitress woman, Nell, talking insistently to Selina. The girl was shaking her head as if she didn't like what she heard.

'What was all that about?' Vince asked.

Selina frowned. 'She offered me a job.'

'Yes, I can guess what kinda job that was.'

Selina didn't reply and her young companion stared at her, dark-eyed as an adoring puppy. He just couldn't bear to leave the girl.

'Why doncha come with me?' he blurted out. 'I was gonna go tonight but I guess a day off work won't hurt. We could leave in the morning.'

'What for?' she cried. 'There's nothing at your mill for me.'

'No, but I'm sure Doc Blazer could find you a job in the office or his house. The Indian agent lives near by, too. His missus runs a rest house for travellers. I bet she needs a girl to help.'

'Are you sure?' Selina's blue eyes lit up. 'Yes, why not? It sounds a good idea. We'll leave first thing.'

The stove was still alight when they got back from

the saloon and they sat around chatting animatedly.

Selina recounted her life with her father, and Vince described how he had been in an orphanage. When he was thirteen Doc Blazer had taken him in and trained him to be a sawyer. 'I've been doing it five years. It's hard work but I enjoy it. Mind you, he don't pay much, ten dollars a month all found.'

'Whew!' Selina gave a whistle. 'Sounds like you're practically his slave. A cowpoke makes thirty a month and Pa seemed to think they were poorly paid. Maybe that's why so many of 'em turn bad, take up robbin' and rustlin'.'

'Aw, it ain't so bad.'

'No, Vincent, you oughta ask for a raise. You're eighteen now. Money's important in this world. You oughta get your proper worth.'

When it came time for bed she called out, 'You take Pa's bed. He ain't gonna be needing it no more.'

A sheet curtain had been draped over a rope between the two beds for modesty's sake. But as he pulled off his boots Vince could see her silhouette outlined behind the sheet, hear the rustle of her dress and undergarments as she disrobed. He gave a gulp of his Adam's apple as she stretched her arms to throw back her hair. It looked to him as though she slept naked.

'Goodnight, Vincent,' she called as she snuffed the candle. 'I'm glad I met you. You're nice.'

Vince lay there in the dark, his blood pounding through him. How he longed to raise the curtain, to reach out to her, touch her arm, her breasts, kiss those ruby lips. But gradually Selina began to breathe deeply, falling into sleep. Vince clenched his fists in agony.

He had been too slow, too respectful. His chance was lost.

The rain had ceased and there was a refreshing coolness in the air. After riding all day Selina and Vince reached the banks of the fast-flowing Tularosa, one of the upper tributaries of the Rio Hondo. Vince led the way on his scrubby mustang, while Selina rode astride her late father's yellow bob-tailed nag. Her skirts were hoisted up about her lissom thighs and she gloried in the sight of the setting sun, the clear roseate sky, now that the storm had blown away, the reflected colours of reds and silvers of the cliffs as they wove their way through the mountains. In some ways it was good to be free. 'Free as a bird,' she sang out.

'Doc's gonna be mad at me for missing a day's work at the sawmill,' Vince said. 'But he's a good man. I guess he'll understand when I explain the situation.'

'You sure he won't mind me coming along with you?' Selina called, for they were riding Indian file along the rocky trail.

'No, course he won't,' Vince sang out, and muttered to himself, 'Well, I hope he won't.'

*

Blazer was blazing mad.

'Where the hell you been, boy?' he snarled. 'And who the hell's this little hussy you've got with you?'

It was almost dark as they rode in over the mountain to South Fork where Blazer's Mills was cradled by forest slopes rising on both sides of the fast-flowing Upper Tularosa. Here the millrace was about ten feet wide powering a wheel that ground flour in one wooden building, and also a belted contraption that drove a circular saw in another barn.

Vince tried to explain the sad circumstances that had kept him at White Oaks. 'Selina's daddy was shot dead by Jake Blackman, sir. It was my Christian duty to stay and give her support at his funeral.'

'Your Christian duty,' Blazer sneered. 'Since when have you been so devout? Your duty to this unfortunate wench involves bringing her back here, does it? And what exactly will her duties be? Oh, aye, I can see what you have in mind for her.'

Dr Joseph Blazer was not normally an unkind man. But he had had a trying day fullfilling an order for planed planks and the belt had been playing up. 'You think you can just skip your duties on account of some bit of skirt you've bumped into? Where, pray, did you meet this Mexican maiden?'

'She's not Mexican, sir. Her father was a white gentleman from Kentucky. It was in the Longhorn saloon.'

'Oh, yeah, I kinda guessed saloons might come into it. So what was the girl doing in the saloon that caught your fancy, Vincent?'

'She was dancing, sir.'

'Oh, she's a dance gal in a saloon who kinda got your longhorn twitching, eh, boy? Well, I can sure see what you're after. You'll be at her up in the hayloft when you're s'posed to be working, eh, Vincent? Won't be long 'fore this pretty li'l Mex 'breed'll have a bun in the oven. So, who's gonna look after her then? You? Or me?'

'It ain't like that,' Vince protested. 'I ain't gonna do no such thing.'

'He certainly ain't,' Selina agreed, as she sat her horse and indignation boiled up in her. 'I'm a decent girl. I keep myself to myself. I don't want no man touching me. Vincent said you might be able to give me work and accommodation and that's all I'm asking. I ain't got no other place to go.'

Blazer, a former dentist which accounted for his 'doctor' prefix, was a tall, stern-looking man with a face like a hawk about to pounce, a crest of stiff hair sticking upwards from his scalp. 'Well, maybe you better go back to your dance saloon, young lady. You're sure to find some gentleman willing to take pity on you there.'

'I know where I ain't wanted,' Selina cried, turning her horse, 'I'll go back to White Oaks. No need to worry 'bout me, Vince.'

'Aw, step down and come inside,' Blazer shouted. 'I wouldn't kick a dog out this time of night. You need to eat and stay the night. But, I'm sorry, Selina,

34

there's no work for a gal here. In the morning Vincent will see you back to White Oaks.'

'I'll go now,' Selina pouted.

'That wouldn't be a bright idea,' Joseph Blazer said. 'This is my house. That other big one over there I rent to the Indian agent, Mr Godfroy. His wife will put you up tonight. Those mountains over there, that's the domain of the Mescalero Indians. And don't believe those tales that the Apache don't ride at night. Moon's fit to rise. They could well be on the prowl looking for mischief.'

'Maybe you'd better go see Mrs Godfroy,' Vince said.

'Yes.' Selina quickly slid from the bobtail. 'Maybe I should.'

Selina was none too pleased when Vince found her in the morning. Mrs Godfroy had no need of a girl. Her grown daughter helped with the chores. She had told Selina to sleep in an adjoining shed. 'The tacky old cat charged me a dollar for supper and horse feed,' the girl complained, as she tugged a comb through her hair. 'Don't think I'd want to work here, anyhow. Look at that dirty ol' mattress I had to sleep on. Folks sure ain't very hospitable around these parts.'

Vince nodded glumly. 'This is where Billy and his gang killed Buckshot Roberts. Charley Bowdre got him in the chest an' he took refuge in here. That's prob'ly the very mattress he lay on by the open door to keep 'em at bay with Doc's Winchester. Yes, there's the bloodstain. They let him bleed to death. I saw the whole thing.'

'Charming,' Selina said, as she packed her carpet-bag. 'No need for you to lose another day's pay, Vincent. I'll find my own way back.'

'No, I've told him I'm taking you. I got the hosses saddled.'

'Good. Sooner I'm outa here the better. Them mice didn't give me much sleep.'

They rode their horses up high along precipitous sheep trails on the edge of the Sierra Blanca range, proceeding in silence for four hours or so until they paused to rest the mounts and admire the view.

'Look, see those houses in the haze about twenty-five miles away? That's Lincoln. That stream there sparkling in the sun's the Ruidoso where Charley Bowdre had his ranch. Sheriff Garrett killed him at Stinking Springs.'

'Goodness! It don't sound very safe around here.'

'No, it ain't. Down there's Eagle Creek and beyond you can just see Fort Stanton. Most of the soldiers are blacks. They're s'posed to be here to keep the Apaches in order. But that's another cause of trouble. Folks round here don't like being ordered about by one-time slaves.'

He made a small fire to boil up coffee, and gave her a chunk of cornmeal loaf to eat. 'This is tasty,' Selina said.

'It's got chesnuts in it. Mrs Godfroy bakes it.'

'Oh, *her*,' Selina muttered, as she sat on a rock and chewed. 'I didn't much care for her stuck-up daughter, either. Smirking like a cat who's got the cream. She told me she was Billy's sweetheart.'

'She mighta been one of 'em. Strikes me he had quite a good few,' Vince remarked, with a touch of envy. 'He was quite a ladies' man.'

'Well, he's dead now, so it didn't do her much good. How much further we got to go?'

'About twenty-five miles. You can see the smoke of White Oaks to the north. Look, there's the trail from Lincoln winding up past the big hump of El Capitan towards it. Hey, that's the stagecoach going up there.'

'Maybe we should hold it up,' Selina suggested, in a low voice. 'Seems to me that's the only way we'll ever get rich.'

'Maybe we should,' Vince muttered, for although he was a law-abiding youngster, she had planted a seed in his mind.

When they reached the Murphy ranch there was a clear trail for ten miles to the mining town. 'You'd better go back now, Vince. I'll be OK from here. Go on, you got a long ride.'

It tore him apart to let her go. 'I'm sorry,' he stuttered. 'I . . . I've caused you trouble. I don't like to think of you on your own.'

'I'll be fine, don't you worry about me.' She opened the carpetbag. 'Here, why don't you have Pa's pistol. I don't want the heavy ol' thing. A man needs protection, seems to me.'

'So do you, Selina.'

'I got his li'l derringer.' She smiled. 'That's good enough for me. I'll go now. I don't like goodbyes.'

He watched as she headed bravely off on the bobtail along the trail. 'I'll ride over next Sunday,' he shouted. 'Don't go forgetting me.'

Selina waved gaily, and Vince grinned, examining the Navy Colt. He touched the trigger, and he and his horse jumped with alarm as it exploded and a bullet ricocheted off a nearby rock. 'Jeez, I better be careful with this dang thing.'

The girl had turned and he waved to her again. He watched as she cantered on to disappear round a bend in the trail. 'I'll go look for her again,' he whispered. 'I don't care what Doc Blazer says.'

# FOUR

'I'm going after them two murderin' hoss thieves,' Pat Garrett said, the morning after Cotton Bulloch had ridden in. 'My deputies are out collecting taxes up White Oaks way. You wanna come along?'

'It ain't federal business.' Bulloch had spent the night on one of the deputies' bunks above the cellar of the courthouse, where they kept prisoners. He was beginning to get an inkling of the workings of lawmen. And he had a good idea what Garrett was really after: the Morgan stallion. 'But I don't mind siding you.'

They rode downriver at a fast lope through blustery rain squalls that swept across the country, much welcomed in such a dry land. In his saddle-bag Garrett had the final eight chapters that he had scribbled of his manuscript, *The Authentic Life Of Billy the Kid*.

When they reached the small settlement of Roswell, he proudly presented it to the postmaster,

Ash Upson, who had penned the first fifteen chapters for him in his florid, highly imaginative style.

Upson was a mournful-looking little man, with a broken nose and face pitted by smallpox. He had wandered all over the States and, like many would-be writers, had a love of both literature and the bottle. 'Hmm,'he muttered, doubtfully, as he scrutinized the pages. 'This ain't bad, Pat, but—'

In fact, Garrett's was the only truly authentic section of the book. 'OK, Ash? Good. I gotta go to Santa Fe on business so when you've checked it I'll drop it in at the offices of the *New Mexican*.'

Upson was enjoying a liquid lunch so they joined him for a snifter. 'This here's Will, a friend of mine,' Garrett drawled. 'We're looking for two *renegados* on the run. One's got a mugful of gold gnashers. Riding a stolen Morgan.'

'They were here last night painting the town red and scaring the local *señoritas* half to death. Took in more'n a skinful of tequila. Saw 'em staggering off this morning, one on the Morgan, t'other on a mustang he'd bought. They were spending cash like there was no tomorrow.'

'Maybe there ain't,' Garrett muttered ominously. 'For them, that is.'

It was tempting to laze a while longer, for Roswell was a pleasant oasis where the Hondo and other streams ran into the Pecos and crops like corn and peach trees grew in profusion. But the lanky sheriff refused another drink. 'Come on,' he growled. 'We gotta catch up with those guys.'

They rode on entering the Chisum ranchlands where the grass grew as high as their horses' bellies. Garrett was glad of a companion for he liked to talk, especially about Billy Bonney. 'I've done folks a favour. Billy was nothing but trouble. My book'll explain that to the public,' he told Cotton.

'Smoke rising from that clump of cottonwoods,' Bulloch replied. 'Maybe we should take a look.'

'Maybe we should.' Garrett tensed in the saddle, thumbing back the hammer of his Dan Wesson Magnum in it's holster. 'And I figure we should go forward on foot.'

They ground-hitched their mounts and ran forward, doubled up, through the tall grass until they reached the copse through which the smoke of a small fire was drifting. Creeping forward Garrett saw the two *viciosos* sprawled in the shade, somewhat hung over, taking a siesta.

'Waal, whadda ya know?' Garrett eyed the powerful Morgan stallion tied to the branch of a tree. 'Wakey, wakey, boys.'

The smaller of the Mexicans struggled groggily to his feet, reaching for his pistol. But Garrett gritted out, 'Hold it right there, you buzzards. Don't make a move.'

The bigger man raised himself on one elbow and gave a strangulated scream as he pointed at Cotton, who had stepped out beside Garrett. 'No,' he croaked, his eyes bulging, 'You are dead. I kill you.

41

Holy Mother of God! He come back! It is his ghost!'

'Aw, shut up. He's as alive as I am.'

'No. He same man.' The swarthy thug's gold teeth glinted in his gaping mouth as he kept his finger pointed and tried to scramble back. 'He wear same suit—'

If he was going to refer to Cotton's shiny red boots, or his big blue bandanna, he didn't have time. An explosion crashed out and he screamed as he rolled to one side and lay twitching his last like a landed fish. Another bullet blew his skull to fragments of blood and bone.

Garrett eyed Bulloch, as he stood there with his smoking revolver. 'What did you do that for?'

'He was going for his gun, didn't you see?'

Garrett's hefty Magnum rattled out death for the smaller Mexican, who twisted and leapt like a scalded cat as the slugs hit him, then he fell back. 'No I didn't. But *he* was.'

As the acrid gunsmoke wafted away, Garrett poked the two bodies with his boot and picked up a goatskin of tequila. 'Too much of this stuff didn't do you boys no good. You shoulda been over the border by now.'

He knelt to go through their pockets and found forty-three dollars in crisp greenbacks in their waistbands, as well as a handful of silver pesos. He peeled off twenty notes and passed them to Bulloch. 'Fair's fair.'

The tall sheriff went to fondle, or try to fondle, the

Morgan stallion, which reared up, whinnying. 'They ain't treated you so well, eh, boy? Doncha fret. You'll be OK now. I'm taking you home.'

'I bet you are,' Cotton muttered.

Garrett wheeled on him. There was something fishy about this guy. Why should the Mex have thought he was the man he'd killed? 'What the hell you doing now?'

Cotton was prising the gold teeth from the fat *hombre*'s mouth with his knife. 'Yuk! Just look at his brains oozing out,' he muttered. 'What few he had.'

Garrett refused Cotton's offer of a couple of teeth. 'Nah, you keep 'em, pal.' He kicked out the fire. 'C'mon, let's go.'

They slung the Mexicans over the two spare mustangs, hitching them tight, and set off back along the plain to Roswell, Garrett riding the prancing stallion.

Garrett dumped the corpses outside the post office, then pinned a piece of cardboard to the big one's chest. 'Murderers, horse-thieves and robbers, killed resisting arrest,' he had scrawled in Spanish.

He gave a *peon* fifty cents to bury them if their bodies were unclaimed by sundown. Then he headed to a cantina to get stuck into a pile of fried chicken and *frijoles*.

'I guess I'd better head for Lincoln and start looking for them forgers,' Cotton said, after they had both eaten and smoked a cigar with their coffee.

'Yeah,' Garrett drawled. 'If I get any news I'll be in touch.'

When the so-called marshal had gone, the sheriff said to Ash Upson, 'There's something weird going on. That guy put the fear of God into that fat Mex. The Mex obviously recognized him, or not *him*, his clothes.'

'So, what did Will say about that?'

'Nothing. He just silenced him.' Garrett sighed. 'Didn't give him a chance. Well, at least I got me a fine new horse.'

White Oaks would never be in the same league or attract so many hopefuls as the California rush in '49, Pike's Peak or Oro City in Colorado, Virginia City, Montana, and, in the sixties, Goldfield, Nevada, or the fabled Comstock Lode from which $400 million in silver would be taken and a few lucky men reap fabulous fortunes. Nor would it ever even equal the pickings from the mines at Deadwood Gulch or Tombstone, Arizona. But gold had been found in small quantities, enough to make it a bustling, if ramshackle town of saloons, stores, hotels and gaming halls which attracted honest traders and miners, and of course the vultures who always hovered in their wake: ruffians, gamblers, confidence tricksters, thugs, fakers, and prostitutes of all ages, some as young as fourteen years.

Cotton Bulloch rode in on the same day as Selina Shawcross returned to the town. He spotted the nubile, black-haired young beauty, slipping from the back of an ugly yellow horse.

'Howdy,' Bulloch drawled, hitching his mount alongside. 'Where can a man get a decent bite to eat in this town?'

Selina gave him her stern, slant-eyed look, tossed back her mass of curls and shrugged. 'Try Rosie's eating house across the way.'

'Hungry?' Cotton grinned at the girl as she untied her carpetbag from behind the saddle. 'Howja like to jine me? Seein' as I'm a stranger in these parts I'd be glad to make it my treat.'

Selina met the lust smouldering in his dark eyes and snorted, 'Yes, I bet you would.'

'No,' he protested, 'nuthin' like that. No strings attached. I've just done some business down in Roswell and I'm pretty flush. I'd just like a bit of company, thassall.'

Selina hesitated as she assessed him again. In his well-cut tweed suit he looked a respectable sort, though she knew you never could tell. But she had had a long ride and was as hungry as a hunter, herself.

'OK,' she agreed. 'If that's really all you want.'

'Sure, on the level.' Cotton beamed. 'You don't know how much I value a purty gal's company jest to chat awhile.'

The gentleman seemed very much at ease: a man of the world, in fact, as he ushered her into the eating house, sat her at a table and called for a bottle of wine. Very much the opposite to Vince, for instance.

45

It was getting late and the candles had been lit as the stranger filled their glasses and clinked his with hers. 'So what do you fancy to eat, honey?'

'I'm not your honey.' She gave a sulky look as she sipped at the chilled white wine. 'Don't push your luck, mister. I told ya, I'm not like that.'

'Well, what is your handle?'

'Selina. What's yours?'

'William,' he said, inventing another alias. 'William Delaney.' He reached out and grasped her hand in his. 'I don't blame ya for actin' suspicious. I rode into town behind you and I guess those lovely bare legs of yourn musta turned many a man's head.'

Selina shrugged and disentangled her fingers from his strong grip, not without her heart thumping a bit. 'I'll try the steak pie followed by plum duff and custard. That'll do me.'

'Anything you fancy, Selina. Your wish is my command.'

'You're certainly a bit of a chancer.' She smiled, flashing her perfect white teeth. 'I ain't never dined with a man like you afore. This is a bit of a new experience for me. How old are you, Will-yum?'

'Old enough to be your uncle. I'm all of thirty. But I like you, Selina. You're very refreshing. I'd like to look after you.'

'I can look after myself, thank you,' she fired back, haughtily. 'Thirty, huh? My, that *is* old.'

'I still got plenty of juice, believe me,' he said, refilling her glass.

The girl had only been allowed the occasional glass by her father in the past, and she giggled. 'I hope you're not trying to get me drunk.'

'Eat, drink and be merry. That's the best motto in the world.' And, as the food arrived, they did just that.

As the stranger sprawled back with a brandy and cigar he drawled, 'So, what do you do, Selina? This must be a tough town for a gal on her own.'

'I ain't on my own,' she lied, for she didn't want him to know that. 'Me an' my daddy we got a room. An' I got a boyfriend. He's devilish jealous so you better watch out. I just got back from visitin' him.'

'Yeah? So, whadda ya do? You got any kinda job?'

'Yes, I'm a dancer,' she lied again, in a sprightly manner for it was true that she was hoping to become one. 'Over at the Longhorn. This is my day off. What you do, Mr Delaney?'

'Oh, I buy and sell . . . horses, stock, whatever I can get my hands on, you know what I mean?' He beamed at her. 'I do OK.'

'I better be goin',' she said, jumping up and grabbing her bag. 'I'm late.'

'Not so fast.' He caught hold of her arm when they were outside and marched her across the street. 'The night is young. Let's take a look at where you work.'

Selina wanted to struggle; she felt as though she were his prisoner as he held her firmly and propelled her across the street and through the batwing doors of the Longhorn. It was as if she could not resist.

The saloon was jumping; the Mexican band were pounding out their beat, the wheel of fortune was whirling, men were gambling at tables or standing lined up along the bar, drinking and jawing. When she burst into the noise and light a group of them greeted her as if she *was* the resident dancer.

'Hey, Selina, show us your legs,' one shouted, as they caught hold of her and hoisted her on to the podium. 'Give us a whirl.'

What could she do? The Spanish guitars were madly strumming, the drum beating, the trumpet blaring. The fiddler tossed her a pair of castanets and the girl caught them, raising them above her head, clicketing away as she stomped and swirled to the beat. The wine had gone to her head and she was spinning, her ruffled dress cartwheeling above her knees, her feet moving like quicksilver as she kicked off her high-heeled shoes while the grinning faces guffawed and roared, urging her on.

Suddenly Bulloch raised his arm and fired a shot into the rafters from his six-gun. 'That's enough,' he shouted, as the music slowed and Selina wound to a halt.

'Hey, what's going on?' The saloon-keeper, Harry Hawke, in his top hat and tail coat, thrust his way forward. 'Who the hell do you think you are?'

In his wake were two heavy-looking bruisers, who stood threateningly on either side of him. 'Put that damn gun away,' Hawke shouted. 'And get out.'

'That girl ain't entertaining you swabs for free.'

Bulloch pointed the Remington revolver up at Selina, who stood puzzled, her head still spinning. 'From here on she gets paid a decent wage. Selina's been offered fifty dollars a week to perform along at the Golden Garter.'

'Fifty a week,' Hawke scoffed, his whiskey-red nose glowing angrily. 'Get outa here, you joker. Chuck him out, boys.'

As one bald-headed bouncer moved in swinging a blackjack at his gun arm the revolver crashed out again. Bulloch coolly shot him down. Then he smashed the gun into the other's face, showering teeth.

Hawke stared with disbelief at the blood flowing from the bald bouncer's chest wound. 'You've killed him,' he said. 'You'll hang for this.'

'Anybody want to try?' Bulloch swung his revolver around at the mob of startled men. 'He attacked me. He got what he deserved. The same goes for anybody else.'

The wine, the dancing, the smoke, the noise, the shock of the shooting was too much for Selina. Suddenly she felt herself going, falling from the podium.

Cotton saw her coming and caught her, slinging her unceremoniously over one shoulder and shouting, 'I'm this gal's manager. From now on she only dances where and when I say. And I get paid up front first.'

He stalked from the saloon, his boots thumping

on the boards, the gun still in his hand as men parted to let him pass.

'Where's this gal live?' he asked a bootblack boy, who was staring up at him with awe.

'I'll show you, mister,' the boy said, and led him off through the backstreets to a stable with a couple of rooms above it, darkened now. 'Her daddy was shot t'other day.'

'Thanks, kid.' Bulloch tossed him a quarter.

He climbed up the wooden steps to a door at the side and kicked it open with his boot. In the gloom he could make out a couple of beds. He tossed the unconscious girl on to one and rolled her on to her back. 'She's out cold.' He slavered over her as he ripped her dress open and reached to grab her breasts. The moon cast light through a window, illuminating her innocent, almost childlike face. Bulloch chuckled and ran one hand down her naked abdomen. 'She's gonna get a surprise when she wakes up.'

He took a cord from his pocket and bound her wrists to the bedposts, tugged off his bandanna, twirled it and gagged her tightly. Unhurriedly, he pulled off his new boots, the coarse tweed suit, and climbed in on top of the lissom girl, hoisting her thighs, then he slapped her face. 'C'm on, baby,' he growled.

Selina heard his voice. What was going on? He was pressed down heavily upon her. A hairy, sweaty, naked man. She blinked open her eyes and in the half-light saw his grinning teeth. Panicking, she screamed, but all that came through the gag was a half-strangled groan. She would have gone for his face with her nails, but her wrists were pinioned. She writhed to escape from under him, flailing her naked legs, but he chuckled gruffly. 'Yeah, you wildcat, fight. It won't do you no good.'

*Oh, no. Please, no.* Wild thoughts hammered her mind. *No. Not this.* She struggled desperately but there was no escape. He'd got her, that was true. She was pinned down like a wriggling tadpole, his strong hands were pulling her apart. There was no way of stopping him doing what he was doing. Her muffled scream as he thrust himself up into her sounded like a retch of nausea. At the same moment Selina knew that she was trapped, that her life would never be the same again, that he had claimed her.

# FIVE

Jake Blackman didn't believe in banks. They too often got robbed or went bust. He counted out his cash in coins and notes, separating the forgeries he had used in the poker game with Aaron Shawcross from the good notes, and the gold and silver the Kentuckian had put in to the game. He folded the forgeries and tucked them in his pocket to pass again. The good money he poked into an earthenware pot, securing it with rag and string tied tight.

'Thar.' He scratched at the black hairs on his long wolflike jaws. 'Now I'll go find a nice li'l hidey-hole up in the rocks.'

There was nothing he particularly wanted to buy. He just liked avariciously counting his cash, that was all, knowing he had it hidden.

The sun was rising, burning away the mist that hung over the ramshackle cabin and the corrals of horses beside it, the few scrubby cattle tucked away in a maze of ravines behind the hump of the Capitan range. He was in the bedroom and he could hear the shrill voice of his wife, Abigail, as she stirred the breakfast gruel in a cauldron on a stove in the kitchen and bantered words back and forth with a couple of the men. He didn't want her to know what he had in his hidey-hole or she would be nagging him to take her to town to buy her a new frock, or ribbons, or hat, or some such foolery. He thrust the pot into a haversack and slung it over his shoulder.

'Well, look who it ain't,' Abigail cawed. 'Jake's finally managed to git his arse outa bed.'

'Hold your tongue, you leathery ol' bitch.'

The two men, Trick and Newt, in their dusty, down-at-heel clothes, cackled with laughter. Jake and his woman had been together a long time and, as could be seen, there was little love lost between them. They waited for Abigail to give him the rough edge of her tongue, but she just shrugged and spooned out the gruel into three bowls, clattering them down on to a table. 'Thar, hope it chokes ya.'

Jake sat down with the two men as three snotty-nosed children, a girl and two boys, ran in and tugged at their mother's skirts. 'Quit your whining,' Abigail cried, 'or you won't git none at all.'

She had been a good-looking woman once but had grown scraggy and gaunt, her once well-developed bosom losing the battle with gravity and now reclining somewhere in the region of her navel beneath the dirty, spotted blouse. Her feet, beneath the heavy skirt, were encased in hobnail boots. As the men sucked at their gruel she studied them and yelled, 'So when you gonna mend the hole in the roof?'

'It ain't gonna rain no more,' Jake muttered. 'That storm was just a freak.'

'You're the friggin' freak,' Abigail whined. 'You're loaded and we still live in this dump.'

Jake pushed his plate away, grabbed his black hat and got to his feet. 'Boys, give her a hand to mend the roof, then she might shut up. I gotta go along to the mine.'

'Sure, we all know where you're off to, like a friggin' jackdaw to hide your cash in a hole,' Abigail shrieked. 'Don't think I don't know. Where's some housekeeping? When are you taking us into town? These kids have got no shoes. Ain't you ashamed?'

Jake slammed the door on her and, as he was saddling his horse, shouted at another of his men, optimistically christened Pliny, who was coming in for breakfast, 'You got them cattle branded yet? I wanna see it done by the time I get back.'

He rode off along the ravine, coming out on the side of the mountain. He pulled the horse in and looked around furtively, to make sure he had not been followed. He jumped down, climbed up to a rock and poked the pot of money into a hole behind it. 'There,' he muttered with satisfaction, 'that'll be there for a rainy day. Ha! I jest told her we ain't gonna get no rain. Well, she certainly ain't gonna git her thievin' hands on my loot.'

Blackman made his way onward for several more miles, heading up a canyon until he came to what apeared to be a run-down mine. He hitched the horse to a rail beside two other mustangs and stooped low to enter the dark hole of a tunnel. 'Anybody home?' he grated out, as he headed towards the flicker of lamplight.

'Morning, Jake.' Benny Brunelli was a broad-chested, but stumpy little man, only about half Blackman's height. He had a shiny, bald dome, what hair he had hanging down to the nape of his neck in greasy curls. He wore a green eyeshade, his corduroy trousers were held up by elastic braces over his striped shirt. He was bent over a crude printing press and around him were tables of the tools and materials of his art – for artist he considered himself to be: buckets of acids, paints and etching plates.

'How about this one?' he exclaimed with delight, peeling from the frame what appeared to be a ten-dollar note. 'This is better, huh? Not so fuzzy as those others. Did you get rid of them?'

'Well, I did, but then I won most of 'em back.' Jake pulled the wad out of his pocket. 'They were kinda circulating round the saloon.'

'That's no good, just passing them in White Oaks,' Benny scolded him. 'You gotta go further abroad, spread them wide, Lincoln, Mesilla, so forth. Otherwise they'll be on to us.'

'I got other thangs to do than passing forged notes,' Jake growled. 'I got a ranch to run.'

'Benny's speaking the truth, Jake,' the other man, named Mick, put in. 'Spread 'em wide. The boys from Santa Fe will be on to us if we don't.'

'You keep your nose out of this. You're s'posed to be out on guard, not idling about in here.'

'You can ditch those others,' Benny said. 'We'll concentrate on these. Ten dollars is an easier note to pass. Look at the colouring on this.' He held the note up to the lantern. 'Nobody's gonna spot these beauties. Come on, Jake, pull your finger out. You're getting 'em cheap enough.'

'What about Dan Diedrick's big order? Thirty thousand dollars?'

'They're ready. That pile over there. But I'm not happy. I'll burn 'em. Don't worry, I'll soon knock out thirty thou' in nice new tens.'

'Burn 'em? You're crazy.'

'Look, they're no good. We don't want trouble. This is a dangerous game. If things do get too hot I'm gonna have to be moving on. We could get a ten-year stretch for this. Washington don't take kindly to people imitating their notes.'

'*You* could. You're the forger,' Jake slapped the the little guy on the back and grinned. 'I'm just one of the small fry.'

'Don't be so sure about that,' Benny replied grimly. 'You're part of the organization. Those guys'll take out whoever they can.'

'OK. Give me the tens. I'll get the boys to fan out far and wide. Nobody ain't gonna catch us.'

'Right,' Benny said. 'I'll work here 'til about three, then I'll come back to the ranch. You tell Abigail to get me something in the pot for supper worth eating, not her stinking gruel.'

'I'll tell her, but you know what she's like. In one ear and out the other.'

Cotton Bulloch had shaved off his beard, washed, dressed in his suit and was giving his red boots a buff as he glanced at the girl sprawled on the bed, her dress still rucked up around her thighs. 'You promise not to scream I might take that gag off.'

She nodded, frantically, her blue eyes tearful, peering through her bedraggled hair. Cotton knelt beside her and patted her hip. 'It's all over now. What's done's done. No use crying over spilt milk, so to speak. So I don't want you rushing out crying rape. It won't do you no good. You're my gal now, my property. You better get that into your head. The sooner you accept that the better it will be.'

Selina nodded abjectly, and when he untied the bandanna she gasped. 'I ain't gonna scream. Please, mister, untie my hands, too.'

Cotton spotted her father's Bible on a shelf. 'Here, 'fore I do, you swear on this.'

She gulped, hesitating. 'Swear what?'

'Touch it with your hand. Say after me. I swear before God that I will not give evidence against my man, William . . . er . . . Delaney. Come on, say it.'

'I swear,' she stuttered, 'I will not give evidence

57

against you, Will-yum—'

'I swear on the Bible I will do whatever William tells me to do, will work for him and be his faithful and obedient and loving girl. . . .'

'No, I cain't.' She turned her head away as if trying to escape the Bible's touch. 'I just cain't. I hate you for what you've done.'

'Swear it,' he ordered. 'If not, stay tied up.'

He got to his feet as if to leave. Then he pulled the marshal's badge out of his pocket. 'You got to swear you ain't seen this. Or tell anybody I'm a federal man. I'm here working under cover, Selina. I'm licensed to kill. I can do what I like with you, snap your neck, if necessary, nobody can touch me. You understand?'

She nodded. 'Please, just untie me.'

Cotton jabbed a finger at her. 'You should be grateful to me. I'm gonna promote your career. Where else you think you're gonna go? You're soiled goods, baby. No decent man'll want you. You'll get nowhere on your own. You're only fit for the whore-house. You want to be thrown to them black soldiers? No? Well, it looks like you're stuck with me, don't it?'

Selina nodded again. 'I don't 'spect anybody to help me now. Not in this town.'

'Good.' He sat on the bed and unknotted the cords from her wrists. 'I trust you, kid. You're gonna be OK. Just don't try anything, that's all.'

Selina eased her wrists, smoothed her rumpled, bloodstained skirt, and stealthily got to her feet, wary, as if expecting him to change his mind. 'I gotta go to the privy. Is that OK?'

'Sure. Light the stove. Boil up hot water. Have a good soak. I'll be back later. Then we'll go out, see about getting you that dancing job. We'll have a good time. Go on. Off you go. Just remember what you've sworn to.'

'There's that guy!' Nell peered through the murky glass window of the Longhorn saloon and watched Cotton Bulloch walk along the wheel-rutted street. 'He's going in the Golden Garter.'

Harry Hawke, in his shirtsleeves, hurried across. 'Hell! I thought he was bluffing.' The owner of the Garter was by way of being his most bitter rival. It was a more upmarket gaming house, which attracted the high rollers.

'What am I gonna do about that guy?'

'Kill him,' Nell replied, drily. 'Send for Jake and his boys.'

'No, I ain't so sure Jake could take him. He looks like one of them fast guns outa Dodge City or someplace. Who the hell is he?'

'He's got a damn nerve coming in here and killing Bert like that without the slightest provocation. Maybe you should send for Sheriff Garrett?'

'No, I don't want him coming up poking his nose in here. It would only mean more trouble.'

On the previous night he had had to quell a mob of angry customers who had demanded some sort of justice. 'No!' Harry had raised his hands, calming them. 'Bert shouldn't have gone for him like that. He asked for it. I figure that fella was within his rights.'

'But what about Selina?' one had shouted. 'What right has he got coming into town and taking her like that?'

'Selina is a spunky gal. She ain't gonna be ridden over roughshod. Don't worry, boys. I'll get her back.'

Guns and whiskey, an explosive mixture, was easily available in these parts of New Mexico. Death was often the outcome when men flared up over a card game, or harboured jealousy over land and water rights, mining claims, or a woman. Few of the culprits were ever arraigned on charges of homicide, and if they were prosecuted judge and jurors alike were frequently threatened and intimidated.

The only reason the Kid had been arrested was because he challenged the higher authorities, murdering not just a sheriff but, later on, two deputies to escape custody. He had gone too far. Cotton Bulloch was aware of this when he shot the bouncer and was confident that his new 'identity' would give him Pat Garrett's protection. He planned to get what he could out of this hick town, move in on the rackets, maybe get a saddle-bag full of the forged dough, then move out fast to pastures new before they discovered his true identity and put a rope around his neck.

When he stepped into the Golden Garter he discovered, however, that the suave proprietor, Justin de Beauneuve, was a more sophisticated character than Hawke. His premises were devoted single-mindedly to gambling; there were no clocks on the walls, the curtains were drawn day and night. In this hushed, chandelier-lit atmosphere, a poker game was still going on from the night before. All that could be heard was the clicking of roulette wheels or gaming chips.

Justin was attired in the fashion of a Southern gentleman, silk lapels to his pale grey suit, a diamond stickpin in his cravat, and his cuffs were not frayed like Aaron Shawcross's had been. He gave Bulloch a curious smile that stretched his pencil-thin moustache. 'You must be the guy who caused the mayhem across the road.' He threw back his jacket to reveal a silver-engraved revolver on his hip. 'Don't come here trying it with us. We ain't in need of no gal dancer causin' a hullabaloo. You better go back to those rowdies in the Longhorn. And the best of luck.'

Bulloch assessed him and nodded, 'OK, I get your drift.'

It was time to put his cards on the table back at the Longhorn. He strode through the batwing doors as if he owned it. It was early morning and there were few customers about. A bartender cleaning glasses eyed him and called out, 'Harry!'

Hawke, with his Lincoln hat perched on his round, rose-coloured pate, hurriedly bustled out from his office, pulling on his frock-coat. 'You've got a damned nerve. Whadda ya want?'

'A glass of your best and a friendly chat, Harry.' Cotton grinned at Hawke and saw surprise and fear lurking in his alcohol-yellowed eyes. 'I'm here to help you out. I got a proposition.'

'Oh, yeah?' Hawke signalled the 'keep to slide a bottle along. When he'd filled two glasses Cotton noticed the tremor of his fingers. Harry slugged his coffin-juice back too hungrily. 'Drink up,' he growled, nearly choking on the words. 'Say your piece and get out.'

Cotton took more time over his drink. 'How much do you pull in a week from this joint, the tables and the bar?'

'What?'

'I want half of it. You need protection. You could easily go the same way as that plug-ugly pal of yourn. I'm willing to provide protection and the services of my protégée, Selina. I understand her daddy was a gambling man, so she knows how to spread a deck and musta learned a few of his tricks. So when she ain't dancing she could be croupier at one of the tables. A high-powered gal like Selina would be sure to pull in the punters. The suckers would be lining up to play with her.'

Harry Hawke swallowed his dismay. Across the room his other heavy, Rudy James, minus a couple of teeth, was watching them. Harry didn't want to lose another man. 'You're crazy.'

'Yes, maybe I am. People say so.' Bulloch carefully finished his drink. 'Crazy enough to kill both you and him over there. I asked how much profit do you pull in?'

Hawke shrugged. 'That depends. I got a lot of overheads. Maybe a hundred a week.'

'Whoo!' Bulloch gave a whistle of surprise. 'So my original offer will stand. Fifty a week for the services of me and Selina. It's a good deal. You'd better think hard about it. That's half the takings from the bar and the tables.'

The slatternly Nell came bustling across, clattering down her bucket and mop and wiping stray hair from her sweaty face. 'What's this bozo want?'

Harry sighed and hurriedly recharged his glass. 'We're discussing business.'

'Tell him to go to hell.'

'Go stick your head up your arse, lady.'

'Don't listen to him, Harry,' she screeched.

'You'd like to consign me to the fiery furnace, would you, cowface? Well,' Bulloch drawled in his Texas accent, 'you two might well be heading in that direction long afore me unless I start getting some sensible answers.'

'Get this place cleaned up, Nell,' Hawke shouted, exasperated. 'It looks a mess.'

'Yeah, snap to it, lady. There may well be some changes made around here when I'm his partner.'

'Hang on, pal,' Harry growled. 'I ain't said nothing about you being my partner.'

'You will. Think about it, Harry. I'll be back tonight looking for an answer.'

# SIX

Selina's thoughts twisted and turned, running up one alley and back down another, nullifying each other. What should she do? Rush out, scream rape, beg people to protect her? Could she go to the preacher? Even his touch would be preferable to being a prisoner of this brute. How could she? She had sworn on the Bible not to. Yes, it had been under duress. But it was the Bible, nonetheless. Had she enough money to catch the stage, get right away from this place? No. He would see her. Even if she slipped away on horseback she knew he would track her down. Sore in body and mind, she was in a panic of indecision, knowing that soon it would be too late.

She boiled up some water on the stove, as he had suggested, and soaked her body in a hip bath, scrubbing herself clean, washing away his touch. She knew he would be back. Who was he? Where had he come from? Yes, she was scared of him, that was for sure. Why had he chosen her?

What had happened to the horses? The thought of them made her venture out. She put on a clean blouse and skirt, brushed her hair and found the poor creatures still tied to the hitching rail where they had been left the night before. This man had as little concern for the animals that served him as he had for the women he used and abused, or the men he shot down in cold blood. She led the bobtail, and Bulloch's mount too, out of sympathy, back to the stable beneath her room, pulled off their saddles and bridles, put them in a stall, gave them water and nosebags of split corn. She hung her arms around the ugly old bobtail's neck, fondling his mane. 'What are we going to do?' she asked him.

Suddenly Selina jumped hearing his boot-tread behind her and his voice rasping out, 'So, been making yourself useful, have you? Come on.'

He took her arm and propelled her up the outside steps to her shadowy room, thrust her inside and slammed the door.

'No!' She turned to him, seeing the look in his muddy eyes. 'Please! Not again.'

'Aw, relax.' The swarthy Bulloch caught hold of her as she struggled, hauling her into him, forcing his mouth on to hers. 'You want to, don't you?'

'No, I don't.' Selina pulled her head away, defiantly. But she knew there was little she could do to stop him as she saw the lechery smouldering in his eyes, felt his virility and power.

Suffice to say he, in the next half-hour or so, tossed

her on the bed, tore off her clothes and took her in all manner of ways, grunting and gasping, going at her like a maddened bull. At last he ceased, slumping heavily upon her, sweaty and hairy and smelling of whiskey from the bottle he had brought back.

'Here, have a swig,' he growled. 'It'll do you good.'

Selina did so, tentatively, hoping it might make her forget. She choked on the fiery liquor.

Cotton laughed gruffly, pushing her aside like a limp rag doll, but a doll with a pounding heart.

He slumped on the other bed, swigging from the bottle. 'I'm gonna have a siesta. Get some sleep. Then we'll go out and eat an' have a good time.'

Soon he was snoring. Selina got to her feet quietly, dressed and tidied herself, then crept to the door. It was locked. The key was in his pocket. His gunbelt was hanging from the bedpost, the Remington dangling in the holster near his head. She returned to stand over him, her heart thumping. She reached out to the weapon with her fingers. Could she dare. . . ?

'Don't even think about it.' His hand caught hold of her wrist in an iron grip. His eyes regarded her balefully from beneath his shaggy hair. 'Or do you want a good thrashing? Maybe I should tie you to the bed again?'

He was a strange man. Towards sundown they went out and he took her to the dress shop, bought her a fine satin gown, off the shoulder flame-orange in colour, with ruffled white underskirts. He bought red ribbons for her hair, and a pair of golden earrings. In the restaurant he ate heartily and she had to admit she was hungry as she tucked in to the venison stew. And the white wine tasted good, too, soothing her senses.

Cotton Bulloch lit a cigar and took his time over coffee. 'You feel better now?'

Selina nodded, sulky and monosyllabic as an angry child. 'Yes.'

'Good. You look a stunner in that dress, baby. So, we're gonna go across to the Longhorn and stun 'em.'

'What?'

'You're gonna dance. And I want you to put on a damn good show. Come on.'

Cotton Bulloch's entry to the crowded saloon, Selina on his arm, a black mantilla modestly covering her hair and shoulders, caused a good many heads to turn and the noise level to drop noticeably as men nudged each other.

'Selina!' an old galoot cried, raising his hands as if to hug her. 'We was wonderin' about you. Are you OK?'

'Will-yum's been looking after me.' She forced a smile and shrugged. 'Yes, I'm OK.'

'I bet he has,' another man cackled.

Bulloch pushed her forward towards the bar and stood, supremely confident. 'Whiskey for me and wine for the lady,' he snapped at the bartender.

Hawke, in his top hat, waved the 'keep away and served them personally, standing before them, raising his glass as men went back to their drinking, joking, laughter and cards and the noise level rose again.

'Well?' Bulloch demanded.

'Let's see how she performs.' The saloon-owner ambled over to the podium and spoke to the musicians. He returned and beckoned Selina to follow him.

'You ready?' Cotton said. 'Go on. Knock 'em out.'

Selina shrugged, listlessly, 'OK.'

Hawke led her behind the stage curtain and pointed to a large, conical laundry basket. 'Get in that.'

'What?'

'We'll carry you on to the podium and you make a surprise entry. It's only a bit of hokum. Go on, get in.'

They closed the lid when she was in and Selina felt the basket sway back and forth as it was carried on to the podium. This is silly, she thought. The music ceased and she heard the saloon-owner shout, 'By special request, gents, your favourite act in town. Gather round. She's special, she's sizzling, she's dynamite, and she'll be performing here every night from now on, the delightful Selina Shawcross.'

There was a stampede for the front row by the miners. But Selina was stuck fast. When she tried to pull herself out the basket toppled over and rolled towards the edge. Harry Hawke had to run forward and help her. 'Come on,' he shouted. 'What you playing at?'

Selina crawled out. Not a very dignified entrance. The musicians struck up again and she went into her routine, spinning and gyrating, kicking up her knees as the miners tried to gawp up her dress. But somehow her heart wasn't in it, the smile on her face was a rictus of 'happiness' that she no longer felt. Oh, she went through the motions but the motions had lost their sparkle. What was worse, she didn't care, was only too pleased when the music wound down and she could stop dancing, to a disappointed smattering of applause.

'You think I'm gonna pay out fifty dollars a week for that,' Hawke blustered. 'You're joking. She used to do a fandango that had all the ol' boys' boots stomping. What you done to her, Mr Delaney? You better come up with something better than that.'

'She's – I dunno – she'll be better tomorrow.' The Texan was flustered, too. He caught hold of Selina. 'What you trying to do to me?' he demanded angrily.

'I could ask you the same question.'

As Bulloch argued the toss with Hawke, she stood to one side, sullen, beautiful but indifferent to her fate. Nobody would help her. That was plain.

'C'm on.' Bulloch took her by the arm. 'Let's get out of here.'

By the time they got back to the room he was seething with fury. 'Think you can make me look a fool? Think you can ruin my act?' He caught her by her hair, dragged her screaming to the bed, threw her face down, tied her wrists to the posts and pulled up her dress.' No bitch treats me like that. I'm gonna have to teach you a lesson.' He whipped off his leather belt and began larupping her.'

Selina had gritted her teeth, not willing to give him the satisfaction of hearing her cry out. But it was the humiliation that hurt her most. In the morning she could hardly bear to sit down.

Cotton Bulloch tried playing the nice guy, giving her coffee and a doughnut for her breakfast. 'You've only got yourself to blame, Selina. You got me mad. Let's see if tonight you can't do it right. Dance like you did that first time I saw you. Put that fire and craziness back in it. Spin like a damn fizzing Catherine wheel. Get them ol' boys' pants red hot.'

Selina chewed, solemnly. 'Maybe.'

'And it would be nice if you could show a little warmth and emotion to me when we make love, not just lie there like a damn corpse.'

'Love? Is that what you call it?'

'Yes, show a little gratitude. I'm looking after you, ain't I? I'm trying to promote your career. You could be a hot tamale in this territory. We could tour, go to Santa Fe, all over. But you gotta put some heart and soul in your act. Promise me you'll do that.'

Selina finished the doughnut, brushed sugar from her fingers and eased her bottom on the cushion. 'An act, is that what it is? I've got to put on an act, for the boys, for you?'

'Yeah.' Bulloch sounded puzzled. 'Why not?'

'I'll put on an act for you, Will-yum, if you promise me you won't beat me again.'

' 'Course not. Not if you don't get me mad.'

'And if you promise to kill a man for me.'

'Kill a man?'

'Yes, the man who cheated my father then shot him down in that very saloon.'

'Oh, yeah? Who is this guy?'

'A lowdown, murdering scoundrel. But he ain't *exactly* like you. He's a dirty, ragged no-good. His name's Jake Blackman. I want my father's death avenged.'

'Well, honey, why don't you do it yourself?'

'I wanted to kill you yesterday afternoon. Oh, God, how I wanted to. I thought if I got your gun I would, but you woke up.'

'Yeah, I sleep like a cat, you better remember that.'

'I couldn't have done it. I know that. I'm not the sort of person who can kill, however much I hate a man.'

'No, some folks can't. You need to have a special talent. Me, I don't give a damn about any man, or woman, either, come to that. If they cross me I kill 'em, without a second thought.

'I know; that's why you could do it. Then I'll be your woman, Will-um.'

'You will?' Cotton's face lit up. 'Consider it done. Where's this bozo hang out?'

'He's got a rackety ol' ranch among the ravines back of El Capitan. Maybe a mine, too.'

'El Capitan, huh.' That was the area where Sheriff Garrett figured the forged notes were originating. 'This character sounds interesting. I'll ride out today and have a sniff around. Don't worry, gal, Jake Blackman is as good as dead. You rest up, take it easy and be ready to put on a big show tonight for them and me. Here.' He poked a ten-dollar bill into her hand. 'That's your share of your fee. Go on, take it. You're gonna be making a lot more than that pretty soon.'

# SEVEN

Photography was in its infancy, improving every day, but still a novelty. Ike Stevens had grabbed the chance of making a living by hawking his big box camera, heavy plates, and darkroom tent, all loaded on to a burro, around the villages of New Mexico. He would set up in some dusty square, and charge fifty cents to every person who wanted their image recorded for posterity. It so happened that he had arrived at Lincoln and, as Pat Garrett stepped out that morning, Ike was beneath his black curtain calling out to a Mexican family, 'Smile!'

'Just the man I was waiting for,' Garrett grinned, for he had heard Ike was heading this way and he had, therefore, delayed burying for a couple of days the stiffie that Marshal Dunwoody had dragged in.

He waited half an hour while the Mexicans kept their fixated smiles and Ike eventually emerged. 'I got a job for you,' the sheriff said 'You better tie your bandanna tight around your nose. He sure whiffs.'

Ike produced a reasonable likeness of the corpse, the man the marshal had said was Cotton Bulloch.

'Right, we can stick him in the ground now,' Garrett said, paying Ike. 'I'll be sending this to the authorities at Fort Worth, Texas.'

When he had posted the photograph off with his claim for the $1,000 reward the sheriff swung up on to the box of the stagecoach, which had rolled in, heading for Roswell, Fort Sumner and all stops north to Las Vegas. From there he would journey on to Santa Fe to make further enquiries at the governor's office. Garrett was uneasy about William Dunwoody. There were odd things like his being so quick off the mark to silence that Mexican *vicioso* and his obvious unfamiliarity with law officers' procedures. He just didn't ring true.

It was a fine morning. Cotton Bulloch had saddled his mustang and set off along the banks of the sparkling Rio Bonito, branching off on a dirt trail that appeared to lead to the little frequented badlands behind the flat hump of the Capitan mountains. There was not much to attract settlers to these ravines. The mountains were dappled with piñons and juniper, but there was a dearth of fertile ground for crops, or grass to support the scrawniest of herds. Lincoln County covered 30,000 square miles, inhabited by fewer than 2,000 citizens, so why should anyone choose to live here? Unless they had something to hide?

Smoke rising in the distance from the chimney of some sort of dwelling alerted Bulloch and he climbed his mount up into the hills to try to get a look at it from the cover of the trees. 'Go on,' he shouted, spurring the mustang up a steep incline. He circled around along a ridge until he was directly opposite a pitch-roofed cabin, sheds and corrals down in the ravine. He swung down, took an eyeglass from his saddle-bag and settled down to keep the place under surveillance for a bit. He guessed this was what lawmen did a lot of the time.

This must be Blackman's so-called ranch, he thought. There ain't no other place around. There appeared to be two or three men branding a few cattle, probably stolen, in one of the corrals. Some scruffy kids played in the yard. And a woman came out to hang laundry from a line.

'Selina didn't say he was wed,' he muttered, holding the slim brass telescope to his eye. 'Maybe she didn't know. Not that it matters to me. That dame'll probably be glad to be rid of him.'

A short while later a tall, skinny sort in a shabby suit and floppy-brimmed black hat came out of the cabin, climbed on to a horse, spoke to the woman and the men then set off along an even narrower trail that led away beyond the ranch.

'Git!' Bulloch jumped back on the mustang and spurred him forward, ploughing down through rocks and shale, leaping fallen trees until he reached lower ground. He crossed a dry gulch, hoping he would not be spotted, and regained high ground on the other side. Working his way along through the trees he managed to keep the rider in his sights.

Bulloch paused when he saw that the horseman was climbing up to the crest of his own ridge. He kept back under cover of a stunted pine and put the glass to his eye again. Black Jake, or whatever he was called, if it was him, had pulled in his horse and was standing in the stirrups, looking around him as if anxious that he might have been followed. 'Surely he ain't seen me,' Bulloch muttered, jerking a British Army Martini-Henry rifle from the saddle boot.

He stepped down and knelt to rest the rifle's long barrel carefully on a boulder, squinting along the sights, feeding a slug from the magazine into the spout. The range was about a quarter of a mile. An easy enough shot, depending on the wind strength, which he allowed for. He would blow the varmint's head to smithereens. 'Hold it there, mister. My gal, Selina, has asked me to deliver you a one-way ticket to hell.'

Bulloch's finger had just taken first pressure on the trigger when the man bobbed his head down. 'Hang on a minute. What's he up to?'

Blackman had jumped from his horse to poke around behind a rock. He pulled out some sort of jug, opened it up, delved inside with his hand for a while, then, furtively glancing about, shoved the pot back in the crevice.

'Now where's he off to? Guess I better follow.

77

Looks like there may be more of interest. OK, mister, you've got a reprieve for a bit.'

Bulloch rode down to the rock and found the pot. 'Well, whadda ye know? My luck's in today. The jackpot.'

He tipped the stash of silver and gold coins and greenbacks into the pockets of his riding-coat and grinned as he jumped aboard the mustang and set off again. The miser's hoard. Wonder what will be at the end of this trail? Aladdin's cave?'

What Bulloch found was the entry hole to a played-out mine, the embers of a fire still smoking outside and three horses tethered nearby. He rode his mustang back up on to the hillside and left him in a gully behind a stand of piñon, far enough away not to alert anybody. He scrambled down a rocky and steep slope until he was directly above the mine, and lay back beneath the branches of a sturdy pine to keep watch.

The sun moved slowly across the sky and it was three in the afternoon when three men came outside at last. Jake Blackman fed some pine knots into the fire and placed a coffee pot on its iron grill to boil.

A surly-looking individual, garbed like a cow-puncher, and holding a shotgun, growled, 'Don't forget to bring more kerosene. It's running low.'

'Yeah, and we could do with another hurricane lamp in there.' Benny Brunelli rubbed at his eyes. 'I can't get a good look at what I'm doing. No wonder this ain't my best work. I've had enough for today,

Jake. I'll come back with you.'

'Can't you send one of the others to relieve me?' The 'puncher laid aside his shotgun and filled three tin mugs with coffee from the pot. 'It's damn boring out here with nothing to do on my own all day and night.'

'You're getting paid well to guard this mine, Mick.' Blackman slurped at the scalding brew. 'I can't tell them other two. You know what they're like. Soon as they got a few whiskeys down their necks in the Longhorn they'd be spilling their guts to whoever listened.'

'Yeah, well, I'm going stir crazy. How about bringing me a bottle? Or I could do with a curvy dame to help pass the time.'

'Who couldn't?' Benny cackled and tossed a saddle over his bronc, reaching underneath to cinch it tight. His legs were so short and stumpy he could hardly reach for the saddle horn. 'Give us a leg up, Mick.'

The little guy was hoisted aboard and sat perched on his mount like a jockey. 'I'll bring you one of the dogs, Mick. You can talk to that.'

'You keep your eyes peeled,' Jake shouted, as he swung on to his horse. 'If any stranger comes nosing around don't ask questions, just let him have it.'

'Sure,' Mick muttered, as he watched them go. 'It's all right for you.'

He lay the shotgun aside and pottered around, slicing smoked bacon into a frying pan. Its scent wafted past Bulloch's nostrils as it began to cook. To avoid a swirl of smoke Mick stood back by the entrance to the mine. Bulloch had his lariat coiled in one hand, its end wound around a bough of the pine. He dropped the noose neatly over Mick's head and jerked it tight.

'What the divil—?' The guard gasped out as, clutching at the rawhide rope around his throat, he was hoisted high.

Bulloch fixed the rope end tightly to a stump of the tree to hold his victim five feet above the ground, slithered down, and, grabbing Mick's kicking legs, pulled on him with all his weight. 'Heigh ho, here we go,' he called, grinning up at the purple-faced Mick. 'Going . . . going . . . gone.'

The guard had passed out, mouth open, tongue lolling out, his arms ceasing to flail; he looked remarkably peaceful. 'Pleasant dreams,' Cotton said, giving him a final tug.

He reached up and removed Mick's keys from his pocket, then went into the mine. Iron bars, like those of a prison cell, had been placed in the entrance. Bulloch unlocked the gate and stepped through.

'This must be my lucky day,' he crooned, as he examined the wads of forged greenbacks on one of the tables. 'Hell! There's thousands,' he muttered. 'All in twenties.' He took them outside and stuffed them in Mick's saddle-bags. 'Hmm?' He spied the frying pan, warmed up the bacon, supped a cup of coffee and enjoyed the repast. 'Kind of you to have my supper ready,' he quipped to the corpse.

The Texan took another look round, examining the printing press with some curiosity. 'I'd make a damn good marshal,' he said. 'Tracked them down to their lair.' He slung the saddle-bags over his shoulder and went to find his horse. Once he had circumnavigated the rundown ranch, hoping that he wouldn't be seen, he would hightail it back to town. 'I'm in the money,' he croaked, giving a guttural laugh. 'And there's more where this comes from. I just cain't go wrong.'

When William Delaney told her he would be away all day Selina's thoughts turned again to the possibility of escape. She had heard that one of the sheriff's deputies, Hank Andrews, was in town trying to rustle up taxes. A hulking, slow-witted fellow, she knew he would be no match for William's cold-hearted guile, but perhaps he could relay her predicament to Pat Garrett, and maybe he would help.

White Oaks was bustling, its higgledy-piggledy. main street lined with false-fronts and lean-tos displaying crudely scrawled signs proclaiming all sorts of services. A gory depiction of a big bleeding tooth indicated a dentist's, a striped pole a barber's, a picture of a cow the meat market, and so forth. There were also from a grain store to a Chinese laundry, a gold-assayer to the Wells Fargo office, billiards halls and sundry saloons.

The town was seething like an ants' nest, wagons

were being unloaded, sacks of flour, cans of molasses, barrels of apples and beans were being rolled into stores, and a team of twenty mules was ploughing in through the mud, drawing a double wagon of kegs of Slitscher's Dutch lager. The skinner was cracking his long bullwhip and yelling loud profanities. He had come all the way from the railhead at Las Vegas and no doubt was looking forward to swallowing a gallon of his own beer.

Elmer Snow was sitting on the sidewalk, trying to hold a trumpet between his knees and emitting a discordant tune. He had had both his arms amputated after the Battle of the Rosebud in '76. A former company bugler, he knew most folks in town.

'You seen Deputy Andrews?' the girl asked, dropping some silver coins into his hat.

'He's gawn back to Lincoln. Caught the stage today. He said Sheriff Garrett's had to go to Santa Fe.'

'Oh, that's a pity.'

'You wanna catch up with him, next stage won't be leaving for three days.'

'No, it was Mr Garrett I really wanted to see.'

'Anything wrong?' the young beggar asked. 'Maybe I can help.'

'No.' She glanced at his arm stumps, not a lot of good in a fight. 'It's not important.'

'You dancing tonight, Selina?'

'Yes.' She gave him a bright smile. 'I probably am. Maybe I'll see you in the audience, Elmer.'

'Yee-haw!' he yelled. 'You sure will.'

There was a motley bunch thronging the town, including settlers in broadcloth and stout boots, their wives in long home-spun skirts and sun bonnets, mingling with *vaqueros* up from Mexico, cowpunchers and miners in their dusty clothes.

After making a few purchases Selina returned to the room. She wanted to take the bobtail out for a gallop. It would clear her mind. Half inclined to head for Blazers Mills, after five miles she slowed and turned back. What would be the use? She decided instead to write a letter to Vince and get it in the post.

Selina had to admit she loved dressing up. She sat before the mirror, brushing her jet-black hair until it glowed, dabbing a touch of powder to her face, pinning on the golden earrings through her pierced lobes, and fixing the necklace around her slim throat.

She was still there in her rustling, flame-coloured dress when Cotton Bulloch stomped in in his riding boots and long duster coat. He tossed his low-crowned Stetson away, pulled clumps of notes, handfuls of silver and gold coins, out of his pockets and flung them on to the bed.

'What you done now?' the girl exclaimed. 'Robbed the bank?'

'Nah. Finders keepers. This li'l lot was sitting around just waiting to be picked up. Come on, gal,

I'm hungry. Let's go out celebrate.'

He threw off the topcoat and brushed down his suit, giving his red boots a polish. He poured water out from a jug into a bowl. 'I'll just have a quick wash.'

When Selina stood to reach for her shawl, he caught hold of her in his strong embrace and kissed her deep and long on the lips. She had given him her promise, so she did not try to twist away from his mouth. And, anyway, she kinda liked it. In spite of his callous brutality, Bulloch knew how to handle a woman.

'I know what you like, don't I, honey?' he growled at her in his husky voice. 'I know what you *want*.' He picked up a handful of forged notes and coins, still holding on to her, and showered them over her. 'What's mine is yours. Do ya love me, sweetheart?'

'Oh, no!' she protested. 'I don't love you. How could I after what you've done to me?'

A look of anger passed across his swarthy face, then he grinned. 'Waal, you may not love me, but you know you want me.'

Selina gave a sad-sweet smile and shrugged. 'Maybe.'

She didn't want to admit it but his animal strength and appetites, crude as they were, the way he played with her body, did arouse her. 'Come on,' she murmured, pressing him away, tossing her hair arrogantly. 'There'll be time for that later.'

'Yeah,' he laughed, 'you need me, honey, in more

ways than one.'

In the eating-house he bought a tuberose to pin in her hair. He poured her white wine, and instructed, 'Sip it slowly. You're only allowed one. I don't want you falling off the stage again.'

'Oh, please,' she protested. 'It's nice.'

'Nope. We'll knock a bottle back after the show. That's if you put some spark in your performance.'

'I will,' she promised. 'Men like Elmer Snow, they want me to, they get a kick out of me.'

'Elmer Snow, who's he?'

'Nobody you need to get jealous about.' She smiled, carving into her venison steak. 'He's got no hands.'

'Well, he wouldn't be much good to you in bed, would he?'

'You always have to be so callous, don't you?' She chewed for a bit then asked, 'Where did you get all that money, Will-yum?'

'Must admit I had to kill some guy. One of Jake Blackman's boys.'

'Jake Blackman,' she exlaimed. 'Did you kill *him*?'

'Nah. I'm gonna toy with him. Take 'em out one by one. By the time his turn comes he'll be shittin' hisself. Don't worry, I'll get him.'

Selina fell silent as she pondered this news. 'Aren't you worried they might get *you*?'

'Those scumbags? Not a chance.'

'And the law allows you, as a marshal,' she whispered, craning forward, 'to just shoot them down?'

'Sure, I told ya. I got a licence. It's open season. Why, you reckon I should read them their rights under the constitution?' He grinned widely. 'I hanged a man today. Always makes me feel good when I hang a man.'

Selina gave a grimace, pushed her half-eaten plate away. 'I really don't know you, do I?'

'Aincha hungry?'

'No, not any more.'

'What's the matter? I'm ridding the world of a few sinners, thassall.' He grinned at her again. 'Freeing them from their earthly troubles, as the preacher might say. Sending them to a happy oblivion. You want me to get rid of all of Jake's revolting brood while I'm at it?'

'What do you mean?'

'That scraggy wife of his and his unwashed brats. Might as well. Those sort, they breed like vermin.'

'No!' Selina was startled. It was the first time it had occurred to her that her father's killer might have a wife and family. 'No, not the woman and children! In fact, perhaps you'd better forget the whole thing. Please.'

'Aw, come on, it's started now. This is what you wanted, sweetheart. Once the wheels are in motion there ain't no going back.'

'The devil's got me now. He's right, there ain't no going back,' she whispered to herself as she prepared to step out on stage.

Yes, she danced, danced like a dervish, spinning, cartwheeling, tossing her hair, her bare feet twinkling across the stage, wantonly laughing, the skirts of the flame dress flying high about her hips, careering perilously close to the edge of the stage as the faces below leered up at her, grinning and cheering, not sure what it was they were so eager to see, but letting them get a good look at her as the music rose in a crescendo and she collapsed, out of breath, and the lusty audience roared their approval. There were whistles and shouts of 'More!' Selina skipped to her feet and threw herself like a swallow out to them to be caught and held aloft by their lustful hands, passed back over the throng.

'OK, boys, let me down now,' she laughed. 'I'll dance again later if you like.'

Cotton Bulloch was pleased with her, opening the promised bottle of sweet white wine when they eventually got back to the room. 'You were good,' he said. 'They loved you.'

'I'm not good. I'm bad, ain't I, Will-yum?' Selina gulped a glass down. 'That's what you want me to be and that's why you love me.'

'Sure, you wildcat. Let's see how you perform for *me* tonight.'

It was as if she were still dancing, her head spinning from the wondrous wine, her body tingling, wrestling on the bed while Satan reared over her, glimpsing his grinning fangs in the moonlight, running her fingers through his thick hair, scratching her nails down his back, urging him on at the same time as she tried to push him away, screaming out, 'I'm bad, ain't I? I'm real bad.'

# EIGHT

The post hack was coming up the trail and turning into the sawmill. Vince assumed that whatever mail was being delivered would be business letters for Doc Blazer. But, glancing through them, Blazer frowned. 'Looks like there's one for you – in a girlish hand.'

Vince, who was out in the yard sawing up some off-cuts, picked the missive from the dust as it was tossed across to him. His heart was hammering. He tore it open and read it through once, then again.

*Deer Vince,*
*I loved meeting you, but please do not come to see me agayn. My life is changed for ever. I am not the same girl you knew. You are sweet and good. Too good for me. I am sold to the devil and can never be reclaimed. If you care for me at all I ask you to forgive me and forget me. I beg you, do not come to White Oaks again.*
*Selina.*

'What the hell's the matter, boy?' Blazer demanded. 'You look like somebody you know's died.'

'Maybe they have,' Vince whispered. He stared at the slip of paper. Its message had hit him like a thunderbolt. What did she mean, *sold to the devil*? What was going on?

'Ditched you, has she?' Doc Blazer surmised. 'Boy, you've had a lucky escape. I knew when I first saw her that saucy little minx was full of female tricks. She's no good to you, Vincent. You've got to forget her. She's got trouble written all over her.'

Vince shook his head in puzzlement, carefully folded the note and slipped it into his shirt pocket. 'I gotta go to White Oaks. I've got to see her.'

He had wanted to go on the Sunday just past, but the sawyer had told him it was impossible. He had rigged a cable up on the mountainside and they were busy felling more logs to lower down. 'I'm due a day off,' he cried, 'for working the weekend.'

Joseph Blazer shook his hawklike head, his expression severe. 'We have too much to do, Vince. I can't spare you. Your duty is to stay here.'

'I don't care about my duty,' the youngster shouted. 'I've got to go.'

Vince turned on his heel and hurried back to his bedroom in the house, pushing past Mrs Blazer, who gave him a curious look. Now he felt doubly bad because he *did* care about his duty. The Blazers had brought him up since the age of thirteen and been like a family to him, the first family he had ever known, but work would have to wait.

He found the long-barrelled cavalry pistol beneath the bed. It was heavy and potent in his hands as he debated how to carry it. He had no belt or holster, only a bit of string holding up his pants. He thrust it into a canvas warbag with a few other oddments that he might need and found the eight dollars he had managed to save.

He studied the letter again, desperately seeking words that might give him hope. She had called him 'dear' and 'loved' meeting him. She thought he was 'sweet and good'. There was not a lot to buoy him up. What on earth did she mean? He dreaded putting the worst interpretation on her words. No, surely she would not do that?

'Vince,' the sawyer put his head around the door, 'come to my office. I need to speak with you.'

When they were seated in the confined space, the sawyer said, 'Now, look, we've raised you like a son, given you shelter and employment. We don't want you to leave, but if you insist on walking out to go off on this fool's errand I will be forced to dismiss you.'

'Go on then, sack me. There's other jobs that pay more,' Vince blurted out, and instantly regretted his words. 'I'm sorry. I know you've been good to me. But I've got to go. Selina's in trouble and I've got to find out what's wrong.'

'If she's in trouble my guess is she must have got mixed up with a wrong 'un. She's chosen him rather than you. If so, there's nothing you can do. I know she's given you a gun. If you take that you're as good as dead. Do you think I want to come to claim your body to bury you?'

'No.' Vince shook his head, wanting to get up and leave. 'I promise you it won't come to that. I just want to see her, that's all, get an explanation.'

'I fear that's not a promise you will be able to keep. Stay where you are a minute, help me out. I was young once, I know how you feel. But I'm asking you, don't throw your life away on this girl. Aren't there plenty of other girls around? What about the Godfroys' daughter? She's a decent, honest female. She'd make an excellent wife for you?'

'Wife? That spotty, stuck-up—'

Blazer laughed. 'Well, there's plenty of other gals!'

'I've found the one I want,' Vince stubbornly replied. 'And you turned her away. You could have given her work here.'

'She's trouble, Vince. I'm warning you. Look, my health's not too good and I'm gone fifty. It's been in my mind, one of these days, when you've reached your majority, to ask you if you'd like to come in with me, be an equal partner in these mills. I've worked hard to build them into what they are and it seems a shame there's no one I can trust to hand them on to.'

This, too, came as something of a shock to Vince. 'I've got to go,' he said, getting to his feet. 'Maybe when this is all over we can talk. Don't think I'm not grateful.'

'Wait.' Doc Blazer stood too, took a ten-dollar note from his wallet. 'Take this.' He offered his hand to shake. 'Be careful.'

His wife was waiting by the front door. 'I can't stop him,' Blazer called. She gave Vince a hug and kissed his cheek. 'Good luck,' she whispered.

He strode to the stable, saddled his mustang and rode out without looking back. If he kept the mustang at a good lope he would be in White Oaks by nightfall.

'Great Jehosaphat!' Benny Brunelli reined back his horse as he nearly rode into the dangling corpse. 'It's Mick. He's committed suicide. I knew he was lonesome but it didn't call for this.'

'He ain't the suicidal sort. Somebody's assisted him.' Jake Blackman was more interested in going into the deserted mine, and he ducked through Mick's legs. The iron-barred gate was gaping open. In the printing room there were signs of a hasty search. 'Holy Jesus!'

'How much has he taken?' Benny came bustling in on his little legs. 'No, I don't believe it. They've all gone. All those twenty-dollar bills we weren't gonna use. He's nicked the lot. The dirty, thieving rat. This could ruin everything.'

'D'ye mean if he's picked up?'

'Yeah. He's bound to spill the beans.'

This was a double shock for Jake. On the way he had stopped to check his pot – telling Benny to canter on and had found his hoard of gold and silver gone.

'Look at this!' Benny waved a piece of paper under his nose on which was scrawled:

KEEP UP THE GOOD WORK, BOYS. I'LL BE BACK FOR MY NEXT PAY-OFF!

'Who the hell is he?'
Benny scratched his thinning locks. 'Beats me.'

They hadn't come up with any answers by the time they had buried Mick in the rocks and galloped back to the ranch.

Abigail was shrilly cursing a jack rabbit Jake had shot as she skinned and gutted it and chopped it into chunks. 'There, git in the damn pot.'

As they came banging in she yelled, 'What's brought you lot back? Dinner won't be yet. It's gonna take hours for this big buck rabbit to cook. He must be a hundred years old. Gonna be tough as leather. Cain't you shoot somethun' better like a nice tender deer.'

'Ar, shuddup, woman. There ain't none round here.'

Jake went stomping back out again to go and question the three men about whether they'd seen anyone suspicious in the vicinity.

'What's eating him? He's like a bear with a bad head.'

'We've had a bad morning,' Benny piped up. 'One way or the other, it strikes me it's about time I packed up my gear and hit the trail for distant parts, like, say, Californ-ee-ay.'

'What's the hurry?' Abigail turned from peeling a carrot to smile at the sight of Benny sitting in their only wooden armchair. His legs were so short they dangled above the ground. 'I've just gotten used to you. Makes a change to see a cheerful face 'stead of that miserable bastard.'

'You must like him a bit. I mean, look at all the kids. And there's another in the cradle.'

'How can I stop him? He's got his condoodle rights. Anyway, there ain't much else to do at nights.'

'Well, you're a good-lookin' woman, Abigail. I can't blame him. I bet when you were young you were real handsome.'

'Lawks! Me? Handsome?' She wiped her nose on her sleeve as she peeled an onion and popped it in the pot. 'You need spectacles.'

'Well, you ain't ugly.' Benny got to his feet and tiptoed towards her. He daintily lifted her long skirt and peered beneath. Then he grabbed her. 'You *really* like me?'

Abigail let out a shrill squeal. 'What'n hell you doin'? If Jake comes in he'll kill you.'

Benny was busy trying to locate her breasts beneath her shirt. 'Oh, they're down here! If you really like me you oughta show it.'

'What? What'n hail are you up to! You kids,' she

shrieked, 'go play in the yard. And don't come back in. Me an' Uncle Benny's busy.'

When the children had gone she drawled, still busy at the kitchen table which was set into an alcove by the stove, 'You'd better draw up that stool. You won't git nowhere from down thar. And pull that curtain across behind ya.'

Benny giggled as he did so, doing as she suggested, climbing up behind her as she chopped another carrot and groping under her capacious and filthy skirt. 'I'm gonna give ya a big goodbye.'

'Lawks!' Abigail gave another squeal. 'You sure are.' They were at it fast and furious and had barely reached a conclusion when they heard the door scrape open and Jake shouted, 'Where are ya?'

'Makin' the stew,' Abigail panted, out of breath. 'Benny's helping me.'

'What?' Blackman roared. Newt and Trick had followed him in and he looked at them in puzzlement, drawing his big Buntline Special revolver from his belt and clicking the hammer back.

'What you got the curtain drawn for?' He strode across and swished it back. 'What the hell's going on?'

Abigail was scraping another carrot. 'Just toppin' up the pot. Why, you fancy one raw?' She proffered him one. 'Nice big 'un.' Benny peeped around her backside, her apron draped over his front, and beamed at Jake. 'I'm doing the washing up.'

'Yes,' Abigail cawed. 'He's more use around the

96

house than you are. A real fast worker.'

Benny smiled. 'I'm a busy li'l bee.'

Jake glowered at them. 'Get on with it then and git that pot on the stove. I'm hungry.'

He scowled at the grinning men as Benny called, 'We're going as fast as we can. I'm fair tuckered out.'

'Y'all quit shouting,' Abigail hollered, as she turned, mopping her face, looking somewhat hot and flustered. 'You'll wake Charley.'

'I got big plans for this joint,' Cotton Bulloch announced as oil lamps and candles were lit and men began to flood into the Longhorn saloon. 'For starters we could do with a few more pretty gals. I been reading about the latest craze over in Paris, the can-can they call it, a chorus of dames hoisting their skirts, kicking up their legs, screaming and whirling. It's a wow.'

'Paris, Texas?' Harry Hawke asked.

'No, Paris, France. It's on t'other side of the ocean. Ain't you never heard of it? We could keep Selina as the main attraction, but a few more dames would bring the punters in. Why not have a whorehouse upstairs?'

'That would only mean trouble.' Hawke adjusted his silk plug-hat and lit a cheroot. 'Since that preacher arrived in town he's formed a down-with-vice God squad. Them traders' wives would be parading outside every night with their banners and caterwaulin' if we had a cathouse here.'

Like many a Western town White Oaks's council had decreed that prostitutes should be tucked away out of sight in a red-light area and be banned from soliciting in the main street, saloons and taverns.

'Let's go take a look along The Row,' Bulloch growled in his husky manner. 'Maybe we can find ourselves a few good-lookers not yet raddled by syphilis.'

Hawke didn't like it, but pulled on his frock-coat and toddled off with Bulloch down to a row of cabins at the back of town where the 'ladies of the night' plied their trade behind scarlet curtains drawn across their lantern-lit windows, some in skimpy attire calling out to passing men from their doorways.

'It's half-price tonight, ducky,' one old crone croaked.

'Yeah, I bet it is,' Cotton scoffed, and pointed to a prettier party with hazel hair and rouged cheeks, not much older than Selina. 'Now, she's a possible.'

The girl was arguing with a skulking, shifty individual. 'No, a dollar's the price. Not a cent less. . . .'

'Piss off, ratface,' Bulloch muttered. 'Show us your pins, sweetheart.'

'What?' she squawked.

'Come on, up with your skirts. We're looking for nifty dancers to join me show along at the Longhorn. Yeah, not bad. You're hired.'

'What are you doing?' Hawke protested. 'I cain't afford to pay any more dancers.'

'You ain't gonna pay 'em. They're gonna make a

fortune for you. And me. Upstairs after the dancing's done. Why should these gals be allowed to pocket every penny they make when we can take our cut of it?'

'But what about the preacher and his wimmin? They'll be banging the drum outside the saloon every night frightening my respectable customers away.'

'I'll deal with the preacher,' Cotton drawled, slapping the Remington that was pig-stringed to his thigh. 'And those tinpot town councillors. Don't you worry, Harry. Them hypocrites can use the back door.'

'What's this all about?' the girl was demanding shrilly. 'You can't just—'

'You're on our payroll now, sweetheart.' There was a threat in the way he patted her cheek and leered at her. 'Grab your gear and get ready to leave. Come on, Harry, let's go pick a few other plums.'

As they pushed through the hangdog, mongrel-like men who were sniffing around the cabins, Cotton explained. 'Ain't you aware of what's going on along in Tombstone, Arizona? What do ye think all that feuding among the Clantons and the Earp clan is about? Money. They're fighting for control of the gambling, liquor and prostitution trade. *Big* money. And the beauty of it is we don't have anybody to wipe out. I've already come to an agreement with that Justin dude. He stays on his side of the street and we stay on our'n. We leave each other well alone.

What could be easier?'

'I dunno.' The ruddy-nosed Hawke tipped his top hat forwards and scratched the back of his head. 'Sounds like we're biting off too big a—'

'Not at all. What's more, we ain't breaking no laws. It's all perfectly legal. I tell ya, 'fore long the Longhorn's gonna be *the* place to *be* in this Territory. We'll be rolling in malooka. Early retirement beckons.'

'Yeah, I only hope we don't retire from lead pizen-ing.'

'Hey, here's a nice little lady. A few grey hairs. But a lot of fellas like the homely body. Go offer her the bait of a nice cosy bed upstairs in our establishment.'

The Longhorn was in full swing, the music thumping, the roulette wheel clickering, punters noisily packed around the faro game and the card tables, while others were roaring their appreciation as Selina brought her fandango to a full stop, a whirl of her dress showing off her shapely thighs.

Suddenly her heart seemed to stop for a fraction of time as she saw Vince step through the batwing doors. He met her eyes and froze.

She skipped down from the podium, pushing the men's eager hands away. 'Thass all for now, fellas,' she cried. 'Let me through.'

Vince stood in his dusty clothes, his warbag slung over one shoulder, silent, staring at her, as if for him time had somehow stopped, too.

Selina approached him, wary as a fox. 'What are you doing here?' she hissed. 'Didn't you get my letter? I warned you not to come.'

'I just want to talk to you,' he said. 'I wanna know what's going on. You – me – we—'

'I'm busy, Vince. I gotta go spin the wheel. I'm a croupier gal now, too.'

'Just for a little bit. Look, there's two chairs free over there. Can I buy you a drink?'

'OK. I'll have a white wine.' She caught a waiter's sleeve as he passed and ordered. 'Now, say what you gotta say and then go back to Blazer's Mill. There's nothing for you here, Vince.'

'There's nothing I want here, except you. I've come for you, Selina.'

She settled herself, catlike, into the chair and contemplated him, sipping at the glass of wine. 'It's too late, Vince,' she murmured. 'Things have changed. I ain't the same gal I was.'

'What do you mean?'

'Different.' She tossed her glowing black curls back, touched one of her golden earrings, stretched out a leg in the ruffled flame dress. 'I'm different. Don't you see? I ain't an innocent child any more, Vincent.'

'I don't like the sound of that.'

'Look, I can't sit here all night. Will-yum's gone out for a while, but he ain't gonna like it if he gets back and—'

'William? Who's William?'

101

'He . . . he's my new friend. Don't think bad of me, Vince.'

'You didn't wait long.'

'I . . . I had no choice. Oh, God!' She saw Bulloch, Hawke and a bevy of painted trollops, pushing into the saloon and knew he had spotted them. 'I'm his property now, Vince. Please go.'

Bulloch left Harry to escort the troupe upstairs and headed in their direction. 'Well, look at *you*,' he said, stooping to kiss her lips, making it linger. 'Just what are you up to?'

He pulled her brusquely from the chair and sat her on his lap, holding her tight. Embarrassed, Selina tried to wriggle free, but could not escape. 'I might ask you the same thing.'

Cotton laughed. 'Now don't get jealous. Those are your new playmates. You're gonna have a proper dance troupe. Don't worry, you'll still be number one. Nobody can hold a candle to you, sweetheart.'

His dark, hooded eyes flickered over the youth. 'Who's the hick?'

'This is a friend of mine, Vince. I knew him before I knew you.'

'Oh, you mean that boyfriend you told me about? The dangerous one?'

'Aw, I was just joking. Vince is harmless. There's nothing like that. We're just good friends.'

Vince was staring at Bulloch with undisguised contempt in his dark eyes. 'So, he's the one who's *claimed* you. I'm beginning to understand.'

'Yeah, she's got a real man.' Selina gasped as Bulloch thrust his knee hard between her thighs and licked, lecherously at her ear. 'And she loves it, doncha, honey? Some useless boy ain't no good to her. So you'd better be on your way, junior. And don't come back. If I see you talking to her again there could be trouble.'

Selina tried to wriggle free again but Bulloch held her close to him. 'I told you, Vince,' she cried. 'Please, you better go.'

The eighteen-year-old youth stared at her and the man for seconds, his hand reaching across into his bag, then hesitating. It was too dangerous. Much as he wanted to kill this man, William, whoever he was, was holding Selina before him like a shield.

'So that's how it is?' he whispered, getting to his feet. Then he turned on his heel and headed for the door, tears of anger, humiliation and torment blinding him.

# NINE

It was a relief to get away from the burning summer heat of the New Mexico lowlands for at an altitude of 7,000 feet La Villa Real de la Santa Fe de San Francisco de Asis, as its Spanish founders had named it centuries before, was pleasantly cool.

Pat Garrett dropped his manuscript into the office of the weekly *Santa Fe New Mexican,* where the editor promised him that a New York publisher would have it out within a few months.

Mightily pleased with himself, Garrett strolled beneath the façade of the Romanesque Cathedral of St Francis, which towered over the city's ruddy two-storey adobes, to the portal of the Palace of the Governors where he flashed his badge and was escorted through the spacious building to the office of Governor Lew Wallace.

Spectacles on his nose, his beard thrust out, Wallace beckoned him to take an armchair. 'I'm just finishing this chapter,' he called out, scratching away with a quill pen at a page which he eventually placed on a pile with a satisfied sigh. 'That'll do.'

His manuscript, *Ben Hur*, would eventually find more lasting fame than Garrett's effort, Wallace was sure, so, reluctantly abandoning the classical world for the more mundane problems of New Mexico, he asked, 'So, what's the news from Lincoln, Sheriff?'

'A lot of scribbling going on down there, too, Lew.' Garrett grinned, glancing at the flask of sherry on a nearby table. 'Thirsty work coming all this way.'

Wallace got the hint and jerked on a bell pull. 'Have you had any word from the US secret service special operative? What was his name, William Dunwoody?'

There was a pause while a Latino maid came in, a plate of lemon biscuits in her hand. She poured amontillado into a cutglass tumbler and passed it, with the biscuits on a silver tray, to Garrett.

'Too early for me,' Wallace said, waving her away. 'I might tell you that the US Treasury Department is extremely concerned about these forged bills being circulated in your area, and also by the failure of Dunwoody to report in.'

'Waal, governor, I have my suspicions about him. He hauled in a dead man he claimed to have found. The corpse had got kinda bloated by the time I got it photographed and sent off a copy to Fort Worth. Since then I've had a telegram from the Fort Worth authorities saying they are unwilling to verify this as identification of a desperado they're after called

Cotton Bulloch.'

'Couldn't they identify the victim's revolver?'

'His revolver?' Garrett played for time, crunching the biscuits and taking a polite sip of the sherry. 'Uh, no.'

'By its registration number, if the man purchased it in a Texan gunshop. Do I have to teach you people elementary detective work?'

'The revolver was stolen by two Mexicans who killed him, along with his cash. Me an' Dunwoody tailed 'em towards the border and caught up with 'em along the Pecos. My intention was to arrest 'em, but this fella Dunwoody was real quick on the trigger. Seems to me he mighta wanted to silence 'em.'

'So, did you get the revolver?'

'Yeah, they both had guns. One a storekeeper's snubnose Colt, t'other a Dragoon .44. They're in my drawer at Lincoln.'

'Good. So, get the serial numbers. Let me have them to forward to Washington and Fort Worth.'

'Yes, sir, I'll do that.' Garrett tipped back the sherry. 'Mind if I help myself to a refill?' As he did so, he went on, 'Well, Dunwoody's already become kinda notorious in White Oaks. He shot down some unarmed bar heavy who tried to chuck him out of the Longhorn, and one of my deputies reports there's a rumour he raped some Mex gal dancer. Whether he did or not, he's set her up as his concubine, it seems, and in public gaze is jogging her on his knee and giving her plenty of them long soul

106

kisses the novelists write about.'

The governor cleared his throat. 'Doesn't seem to me to be the behaviour of a secret service agent.'

'Yeah, well, I thought that maybe he's trying to establish credentials as a bad character in the hope of being invited in to join this gang who are pushing the green.'

'Pushing the green? Ah, you mean spreading these phoney greenbacks. But why hasn't he been in touch? There's a telegraph office at White Oaks. Surely he could send a message in code to report progress?'

Wallace took an ornately headed piece of notepaper and wrote: *Agent X: hand your list of daily notes to the bearer of this message for forwarding to me – L. Wallace, Governor, Territory of New Mexico.* and said, 'Make sure he gets this.'

'Yes, suh.' Garrett nodded, putting it in his pocket. 'There's two dudes I've had my suspicions about for some time, Poker Tom Emory and a guy they call Animal Bousman. They hang around the Diedrick livery at White Oaks. In fact, I got stung, myself. Tried cashing a twenty in the bank at Lincoln – bad money, which was a couple of days after those two sons-a-bitches rode through.'

'Don't you recall who passed it to you?'

'No, waal, it was in a poker game in the early hours and I was pretty well whiskied up at that time of night.' The sheriff took another swig of the sherry to fortify himself, and produced a twenty-dollar note from his pocket. 'This is the very one. You see, it's quite convincing.'

The governor held it up against the light to study it. 'Hmm, not bad, the picture of the President and that sort of thing. A bit fuzzy. "This note is legal tender for all debts public and private." They've got that right. I guess it could fool some folks. But, you see, they've got the name of the Secretary of the Treasury wrong, and of course, I doubt if there's any such serial number. I'll keep this.'

'Do I get reimbursed my twenty dollars?'

'No, I'm afraid not. Sorry, Pat, more fool you. Now then, have you questioned those men, searched that livery?'

'I've had a poke around. That was before Dunwoody, if it is him, arrived. My deputy reports that them two have been greatly in cahoots lately with some no-good called Jake Blackman. Maybe he's in with them?'

'So, who's this Blackman fellow?'

'Aw, some murderin' no-good Missouran. He mainly confines himself to cheatin' at cards, or rustling a few cows.'

'Have you arrested him?'

'Nah, in Lincoln County that's hardly worth the paperwork, as you well know. You wouldn't git a jury to convict, and the varmints he kills are usually of the same ilk as him, so why worry?'

'Have you passed your suspicions on to Dunwoody?'

'No, but I intend to take a ride up there when I get back, see what's going on.'

'Well, Pat, I hope you will.' Lew Wallace got up to stare out of the window at the jagged outline of the Sangre de Cristo mountains against a vivid blue sky. 'Washington regards this as top priority. It would be a feather in your cap if you could solve this case.'

'Yep.' Garrett bared his horsey grin. 'Might do my chances of becoming territorial senator no harm, neither, eh, Lew? I'd sure be glad of your backing on that matter.'

'This is a lovely part of America,' Wallace mused. 'But why is there so much crime and violence here? First we had that Lincoln war, the Kid, and all those killings. Then there was that crazy Quinn woman who went on the rampage last year. Now this. What is it about you people?'

'It didn't used to be like this. We only had the Apaches to worry about. It's since the arrival of the Santa Fe railroad. It's brung all kinda thieves and desperadoes in. Then there's others being run outa Texas by the Rangers, all taking refuge here.'

'I'm hoping not to be here much longer. I'm making overtures for an ambassadorial post, possibly in Turkey,' Wallace remarked, dreamily. Turning from the window he removed his wire-rims and blinked owlishly at Garrett. 'For a former buffalo hunter and bartender you're a remarkably intelligent man, Pat. No need to add that I admire your toughness and resoluteness when going after

109

badmen. Of course, I'll put in a word where I can, but if you've really got political aspirations you should get out of this backwater. Why, New Mexico isn't even in the Union yet. Maybe you would do better for yourself if you returned to Texas.'

'Texas?' Garrett's jaw dropped. 'You mean you don't think I'd raise the votes here?'

'You know yourself you've been cast as the villain of the piece.'

'Yeah, while that li'l runt Billy gits all the glory.' Garrett got up on his lanky legs, and grinned, offering his hand. 'Waal, I guess you're a busy man, Lew. Got your next chapter to write, huh? I'm grateful for any backing you can give me. So, I better be getting on with what I got to do. When will you be visiting Lincoln again?'

'I doubt if that's very likely,' Wallace said as he showed the sheriff out. 'Good to have met you, Pat.'

Azariah Wilde walked from his hotel to the lean-to shed he had had built opposite Dan Diedrick's livery. He had painted a simple sign above: GUNS.

'What can I do for you, sir?' He quizzically eyed the youth with the head of tangled curls who was waiting outside. 'You working over the road?'

'No. I just been bedding down with my horse. I need some shells.'

The little man, who was wearing a smart business suit, unlocked and bustled about inside, checking a rack of rifles. He removed his derby to reveal thinning hair, parted centrewise. 'I see. They're a funny bunch over there. You heard any of them talking?'

'No, I ain't.' Vince reached with his right hand to jerk the Navy Colt out of the warbag slung on his left shoulder. 'Why, what's it got to do with you or me?'

'That's an ancient weapon, I do declare. Must be from 1851.' Wilde took it from him. 'Yes, see, there's the Made in Sheffield mark. Sam had a factory over there. You can't beat the deep blue of good Sheffield steel. Beats our Pittsburgh stuff. No, it's nothing to do with me. It's just that the men who go in and out of there seem an odd bunch. Up to no good, I'll be bound.'

'I wouldn't know. Just give me the shells.'

'They had the shorter claw grip in those days. Harder to hang on to. I'd say this old cap 'n' ball loose powder was converted by the Richards system in '71. A sturdy efficent weapon, but not exactly accurate. Could do with some delicate adjustments.'

'Look, mister, I'm in a hurry.'

'Right.' Wilde handed over the Navy along with a box of a dozen Martin's metallic cartridges. 'That's a dollar. Just what are you in a hurry to do with this killing weapon, son?'

'A man needs a gun, don't he?' Vince slapped down a dollar and grabbed the bullets as he left. He glimpsed his image in the shop mirror. He didn't look very imposing in his straw hat and crumpled jeans. 'Thanks.'

He wanted to leave but he couldn't seem to tear

himself away from the town. He had hung around, hoping to get a glimpse of her. Late on the second night he had been unable to resist venturing into the Longhorn saloon again, standing at the back unseen among the crush of men, his heart pounding as he watched Selina dance.

A troupe of highly-rouged girls screamed and did high kicks, showing off their undercarriages, tantalizingly tossing their petticoats as they pranced about Selina, and the fiddlers sawed their catgut to a screeching frenzy. Many of the miners seemed to be intimately acquainted with the females, calling out to them by their names, yelling coarse remarks, trying to catch hold of them. Selina held her tambourine high, tossing her tempestuous hair, spinning and smiling. But to Vince it appeared that her smile was forced, somehow brittle.

When the dance ended the women jumped down to mingle with the lusty men, some of whom then followed them drunkenly upstairs. So, the Longhorn was now a whorehouse!

Vince saw the big, swarthy Texan emerge from a back room to to claim Selina, pulling the lithe girl into him to lasciviously kiss her lips. Then, with his arm about her, they stood at the bar, drinking wine and chatting. Vince had quickly left, found solace in a more lowdown beer parlour.

He was the only customer there until two men clattered in. He recognized them as the driver of the stage and his guard. They ordered meals and sat on the bench next to him.

'Why so glum, son?' the bearded driver asked with a grin. 'You look like you just lost your love?'

Vince shrugged. 'Maybe I have.'

'Never run after a woman,' the shotgun advised. 'You hang around, there'll be another one along soon enough.'

'Yeah, like our stagecoach service.' The driver guffawed and pulled a bottle from his topcoat pocket. He tipped a shot into the youth's empty glass. 'Have a drink. Cheer yeself up.'

'Sure.' Vince tried not to choke on the harsh, corn whiskey. It made his head spin. The heat from the cooking was oppressive, but he had nowhere else to go, and as the men got stuck into their grub, he let his head fall forward, resting on his arms, and fell into a semi-doze.

Vince had his head turned from the two men and his eyes flickered open as he heard them talking about their next assignment in gruff, low voices. 'Don't worry about the kid,' the guard said. 'He's flat out.'

'We gotta pick it up from the gold exchange first light of dawn. Then we'll take on any passengers.'

'How much is there?'

'Ten grand in dust,' the driver muttered.

'Won't be no trouble. We're keeping it hush-hush.'

Vince closed his eyes and pretended to sleep some more. . . .

Now, this morning, as he stepped from the gunshop, he was gripped by a choking, drowning sensation as he saw her strolling along the sidewalk towards him. She was in an embroidered white cotton summer dress, and a shawl lay loose around her shoulders, a shopping basket hung on her arm. Her shining ebony hair was drawn back tight against her skull, held in a top-knot by a scarlet ribbon. The style emphasized her high cheekbones. There was no doubt about it: she was a dazzler.

'So, you are still here.'

'Yes. I want to speak to you.'

'Why?' There was no longer any merriment in her eyes. 'You know it's no use.'

'I want to ask you something.'

'Oh.' She sighed and tugged at his sleeve. 'Come into the restaurant. It's not safe for us to be seen together.'

'Why are you frightened of that thug?' he asked angrily, as they sat down at a table and Selina ordered coffees.

'He's got a violent temper,' she hissed. 'I'm frightened for you.'

'You can get away. I'll help you.'

'Ha! Help yourself to an early grave, you mean. I see you've been buying bullets. They'll be no good to you. You know you're no match for him. I want you to give me back my father's gun. And go away.

114

Forget me.'

'I can't do that. I love you. You love me, too, don't you?'

'What?' she cried sharply. 'You are a fool, Vincent. Don't you realize, I am his lover.'

'But you don't love him. There is a difference.'

They fell silent as the woman served coffees, and Selina spooned sugar, stirring it into the cream. Her vivid blue eyes burned into him: the eyes of an executioner. She knew she had to be cruel to him to make him go.

'What does it matter?' She shrugged and smiled. 'I love what he does to me. He excites me.'

That hit him. It took a few moments to recover as he gulped down the coffee. 'No. You know you need to be free. You're like a bird caught in a trap. I intend to rescue you.'

'Really? Where would we go, Vincent? You have nothing. What would we live on? We would have to go a long way from here or he would track us down.'

'If I had ten thousand dollars, would you come with me?'

'Ten thousand? Where would you get that from? Don't be absurd, Vincent. Go back to your mill.'

'I'll get it.' He patted the gun in his bag. 'Don't worry about that. Then I'll be back for you.'

'I've heard enough of this foolishness.' She suddenly got to her feet. 'I must go. I'm no good to you.'

He caught her arm. 'Does he make you go with other men?'

'No. I wouldn't.' She pouted her lips, defiantly. 'I'm just his. So leave me alone.'

He watched her go, then called out, 'Selina, I'll be back.'

His mind made up, he saddled the mustang and headed at a fast lope out of White Oaks. Tomorrow he would wait on a lonesome part of the trail for the stagecoach. He was desperate.

# TEN

Co-owner of West and Deidrick's corral at White Oaks, Dan Diedrick had not long been in cahoots with Jake Blackman and had now come up with a plan to smuggle $30,000 of the fake notes into Texas to purchase a big herd of cattle for resale.

'Go see if they got the cash ready yet,' he told Poker Tom Emory and Animal Bousman, who saddled their mustangs, rode fast out of White Oaks and headed through the ravines behind El Capitan towards Jake's place.

Poker Tom was double-rigged, revolvers slung on both hips, for he liked to think he was a fast gun as well as a gambling man. He affected a wide-brimmed sombrero, a tight-buttoned brocade waistcoat over a white shirt and loose bow. His legs were protected from the scrub by shiny leather shotgun chaps above chunky Mexican spurs. All in all, he was a bit of a joker and show-off.

His companion in crime was exactly opposite, dubbed 'Animal' for his lack of any such gentlemanly refinements. He was fat, hairy and unwashed, and it was wise to ride upwind of him.

'Anybody home?' Poker Tom yelled, as they rode into the Pikeys' encampment of dilapidated cabins amid a general array of discarded animal offal, empty bottles, broken wagon wheels and any old litter lying where it had been tossed from windows. Amid all this tatterdermalion brats roamed and a chained cur howled. 'Jasus, it stinks worse than a Comanche camp, or *you*, come to that.'

From a lopsided privy Jake emerged, hauling up his long johns and the filthy trousers of his black suit. 'What you doin' here?' he growled. 'You sure you weren't followed?'

'We've run out of lettuce,' Tom explained airily. 'We spread it through Lincoln an' all the way up to Fort Sumner far as Las Canaditas 'fore it ran out. Dan wants the thirty thou' you promised him.'

He and Animal had done well out of their last consignment, breaking up twenties for small purchases in stores, saloons and cantinas, even splitting them in banks, keeping the good notes and the gold and silver in change for themselves and Diedrick.

'Yuh,' Animal agreed, sliding down from his big bay. 'It was easy. Nobody suspected nuthin'. You got some more?'

'Ain't got no more,' Blackman barked. 'All bin stole an' my real cash with it too.'

It was humiliating to admit that he had been the victim of robbery and murder, just like the innocent victims he had subjected to such treatment on his wanderings.

'When I catch up with whoever done it,' he snarled, brandishing a big axe, 'he's gonna rue the day he ever been born.'

'Yuh, chop off his balls,' Animal growled. 'Who did it?'

'How the hell do I know?'

Three of Jake's sidekicks were coming from the barn and Jake shouted, 'Get the herd ready to go. We'll take 'em into White Oaks.'

He only had ten steers, ten bullocks and two cows, but he should be able to raise more than $200. There was a ready market in the booming gold town for most things, especially stolen beef. 'I'm stony broke,' he moaned. 'Need some ready cash. The bastard raided the mine behind our backs, killed Mick, hanged him by the neck.'

'Ooh!' Animal exclaimed. 'Dat ain't a nice way to go.'

'New Mexico's full of murderin' thieves,' Poker Tom sympathized. 'I don't know what this modern world's coming to.'

'S'pose you wanna sup of soup 'fore you go back,' Jake replied, shambling off to the cabin, shouting at the snarling dog to shut up.

To annoy him even more Benny Brunelli was perched in his wooden armchair. 'Ain't it time you got back to the mine and started punching out more greenbacks?'

119

'I ain't going back there on my own,' Benny howled. 'Not with that crazy killer on the loose. You can't all just go off to town and leave us alone.'

'Abigail will protect ya. She's a dab hand at killin' rats with a shotgun. You can hide under the bed.'

Abigail wiped her nose on her sleeve as she slopped out her infamous gruel into wooden bowls for the men, tossing them hunks of stale oaten bread. It's the fourth of July tomorrow, Jake. Ain't ya takin' us all into town to celebrate?'

'What the hell we got to celebrate, woman? I tell ya we been robbed.'

'Yeah, I bet you got plenty other jugs buried places,' his wife sniped. 'Go dig one up.'

'Duh, lady, dis is nice.' Animal, hairy as a gorilla, was snorting and splurting soup as he spooned it into his bearded mouth-hole. 'Got any more?'

'Not for somebody who eats like a friggin' pig. Whoo, you don't 'alf whiff.'

'What, worse than Jake?' Poker Tom chuckled.

Animal scratched black fingernails at his tattered, lice-ridden vest, and poked with his other grimy paw at bits of bread stuck in his even blacker teeth. 'Nice place you got here,' he said, looking around.

'Is he short-sighted, too?' Jake growled, reaching for his rifle. 'Come on. Let's ride.'

'I ain't sure I'll be here when you get back. I'm taking my stuff in the wagon and skinning out, back to California,' the little forger sang out. 'This racket's played out here.'

120

'Suit yourself,' Jake growled. 'Dan would pay well for thirty thou'.'

They had met in the state prison, where they had shared a cell for a year, and he had recommended New Mexico as a ready market for Benny's artistic talents.

'I'd feel safer back in San Quentin.'

'Aw, don't go. Stay and poke the stove for Abigail,' Poker Tom sniggered. 'Keep Jake's bed warm.'

'We're just good friends,' Benny protested.

Jake snarled at Tom, 'One of these days your smart mouth is going to get you in trouble.'

As the gang trooped out to climb on their long-suffering horses, Abigail howled, 'Go on, leave your wife and children to that murderin' lunatic who's on the prowl.'

Poker Tom tipped his hat to her. 'Have a fine Independence Day, ma'am.'

Vince had climbed high into the mountains and stayed overnight at a sheep camp, where the herder welcomed him with traditional Spanish hospitality to share their meal: tortillas and tough goat stew, peppery hot. While the Mexican and his wife pottered about around their fire Vince attended to his mustang. He removed the saddle and rubbed him down, and replaced the bridle with a rawhide hackamore, paying out the rope so that he could crop whatever he might find amid the cactus and rocks.

The couple's daughter watched him. She was

about the same age as Selina but different in character: shy and modest. 'He is a well-mannered horse for a mustang,' she said.

'Yes, I taught him myself, the Comanche way.'

'What way is that?'

Vince recalled Doc Blazer's words when he had given him the young wild critter and watched him handling it, quietly but firmly, in their corral. 'You can't break mustangs with kindness,' he had shouted.

'Most Americans break a horse by riding, whipping and spurring him until he can take no more,' he told the girl, in the frontier Spanish in which most folks around here were naturally fluent.

'Look at this.' He offered the horse his hand, stroking its head, brushing the flies from its eyes. 'When you start to tame him you mustn't look him in the eye. Stand turned half-away from him. At first, soon as he looks like he might bite or rear you walk away. This puzzles him and he follows you. It's called the yoyo method. You know those yoyos kids play with. You go back and forward and gradually you get him doing what you want.'

'That sounds easy,' she said.

'It depends how you do it. In the wild, a mustang's main fear is of attack by a puma. If you suddenly leap on him, of course, he's gonna buck. You ease a saddle on, slowly, let him take your weight. Next thing you're aboard, no fuss, he's your horse. I can rely on him. We've got a bond.'

122

'That's good,' the girl said. 'I wish I had a horse.'

'You've got a burro.'

'Yes, but my father rides that. We walk.'

'It must be lonesome for you up here.' He stood silhouetted against a blood-red sky as the westering sun sank behind the stark peaks of the Sierra Blanca.

'The sheep aren't much fun,' she replied.

He glanced at the woolly creatures huddled in their brushwood corral for the night, then jumped down to join her. He smiled. 'Maybe that guy was right,' he muttered in English to himself. 'There *are* plenty of other girls around.'

'Will you pass this way again?' she asked.

She was a pretty little *querida*, her black eyes coquettish as she pulled her *reboso* around her. Why couldn't he have fallen for a girl like her? But he knew it was too late. He was obsessed with the wicked Selina.

'Who knows,' he said darkly. 'Tomorrow I might be dead.'

Their *jacal* of rocks was really just a hole in the ground. As he pulled his blanket around him, lying back on his saddle before they extinguished the lantern, the girl looked across and smiled.

He shook his head and stared into the darkness. Why was he going on with this foolishness? But he knew he could not stop. Tomorrow he would roll the dice to lose or win all.

\*

The deeply rutted wagon trail from the mining town wound down through steep-sided mountains girt with stunted oaks and pines. It meant the six-horse stagecoach had to be slowed to manoeuvre its way through. This suited Vince admirably. He leapt down from a ledge of cliff and landed on the roof directly behind the driver and guard. He thrust the barrel of the Navy Colt into the guard's broad back and shouted through his bandanna mask, 'Ditch that gun overboard.'

The guard froze for seconds until Vince growled, 'I'll blast your spine apart, mister.' The guard tossed the shotgun away. 'Right.' Vince jabbed the Colt into the driver's back. 'Haul them horses in, pal.'

When the team had come to a restive halt, Vince shouted, 'Hand over that gold dust. Come on. I know you've got it. I've got an itchy finger on this trigger. I ain't got all day. Move!'

'It's in a strongbox,' the driver replied. 'Under us.'

'Right. You.' He poked the guard again. 'Pull it out and toss it on to the ground.'

The man had to get up to reach down to hoist the iron-bound wooden trunk out and, looking back he glanced at the hold-up man. 'You're gonna regret this, kid,' he warned, pushing the strongbox to the edge and tipping it over to the ground.

'Get back in your seat and shut up,' Vince shouted.

He jumped down. The trunk had fallen into a rut, making it difficult to get at. He managed to right it while at the same time trying to keep one eye on the driver and guard.

A woman stuck her head out of the window, clucking like a disturbed chicken. 'What's going on?'

Vince waved the Colt at her. 'Get back inside, lady.' He aimed at the lock, gritted his teeth and fired. The bullet rebounded dangerously off the metal and ricocheted away. The lock was shattered. But the shot had startled the horses who had started away down the decline. As they did so the guard brought out a revolver from under his coat; grimacing angrily he crashed out a bullet. The slug seared the side of Vince's chest, hitting him with such force that he was knocked to the ground. 'Oh, God!' he cried, struggling to get to his feet.

The stagecoach had swayed on down the trail but was being pulled to a halt about a hundred yards away. Frantically, Vince jerked open the lid of the strongbox and pulled out two pokes of gold dust. He stuffed them in his haversack, but as he did so another bullet whined past his head, making him duck with fright.

Both the driver and guard had climbed from the coach and were headed up towards him, guns in hands, looking like they meant business.

Vince could hardly think straight because of his panic and the burning pain on his chest's side, but he found the revolver on the ground and snatched it up by its claw butt, aiming it their way. He fired several shots to stop them in their tracks. Like the man said, it was not the most accurate of weapons and the bullets flew over their heads.

He had not time to grab the rest of the gold dust. What was the use of it now, anyway? He could feel blood sticking to his shirt, sickeningly. He scrambled away and climbed desperately back up the side of the cliff as their bullets rattled ricocheting about him. Somehow he made it back to the mustang and hauled himself into the saddle, holding his wound with one hand, trying to stop the flow, but seeing, with horror, blood trickle through his fingers. He urged the mustang away. What was he going to do? Where could he go?

# ELEVEN

White Oaks was *en fête* for Independence Day with flags and bunting strung across the main street. The miners, first thing in the morning, were already in a merry mood, exploding gunpowder 'fireworks' and playing other tricks as cowboys from outlying ranches rode their excited ponies back and forth firing six-guns into the heavens.

'Whee-hoo!' Pat Garrett exclaimed to his deputy, Hank Andrews, as they came out of the jailhouse where they had bedded down overnight. 'Sounds like it could be a busy day.'

In fact, it was going to be busier in more ways than the sheriff imagined.

There were already some early customers starting on a bottle with their breakfast as they stepped through the batwing doors into the Longhorn saloon. Cotton Bulloch was standing at the bar watching Harry Hawke count the previous night's takings, with Selina perched on a stool beside him.

127

'Just the man I want to see,' the sheriff announced, joining them at the bar.

Bulloch frowned at him and drawled, 'Howdy, Pat. Any sign of that reward money yet?'

Garrett flicked a finger to a barman to pour him a shot, and sampled it before replying. 'No, there ain't. The Fort Worth authorities ain't satisfied from the photo I sent them that the stiff you brought in is Cotton Bulloch.'

Bulloch looked at him, sharply. 'They ain't? Why not?'

'Just where is it you said you come from?'

'Me?' Cotton laughed. 'Everywhere and nowhere.'

'Couldn't you be more specific?'

The burly deputy, Hank, had taken a stance, fists on hips, as if this was official business. Selina noticed that the gunshop owner, Azariah Wilde, in his tight suit, celluloid collar and derby, touting for custom had set up his display of weapons at a table nearby and, like others around, was listening intently to their conversation. Garrett spoke in a loud voice as if he wanted all those around to hear him.

'I just got back from Santa Fe with a letter for you from Governor Wallace,' he said, brandishing a piece of paper.

In fact, he had caught the express stage, which only stopped in order to exchange horse teams at various stations and had made good time. At Lincoln he had been met by Andrews and, even though it was late at night had decided to go on up to the mining town.

'What the hell's all this about?' demanded Bulloch.

'I wouldn't mind laying odds you ain't been keeping a daily log of your enquiries.'

'Keep your voice down, Pat,' the Texan whispered hoarsely. 'What you trying to do, blow my cover?'

Harry had finished counting. He split the pile of coins and greenbacks with a chop of his hand and slid half across to Bulloch. 'There's your share,' he grumbled. 'Satisfied?'

'It don't seem to me you're too well acquainted with the rules of being a Fed undercover man,' Garrett pressed, still keeping his voice up. 'The governor wants to know why you ain't cabled him. No doubt you've been too busy muscling in on Harry here, raping girls and turning this joint into a whorehouse.'

If Bulloch was ruffled he didn't show it. He applied his burning cheroot to the letter and watched it go up in smoke before letting it flutter to the floorboards.

'The Governor can kiss my arse,' he growled. 'And so can you, Garrett.' He peeled a ten from the wad of dollars and leaned across to tuck it into the shadowy valley between Selina's breasts nestling in her low-cut blouse. 'That's for you, honey. You better go start dealing the blackjack.'

Selina did not move, apart from stretching out a shapely leg. Expanding her bosom and tossing back her hair with a catlike sinuosity, she slipped from the stool to stand, one hand on the bar. 'No, I'm interested to hear what the sheriff has to say.'

'You want a taste of my belt,' Bulloch snarled. 'Do what you're told.'

Selina faced him, defiant and disobedient. 'No, why should I?'

'Like knocking gals about, do you?' Garrett laughed sardonically. 'That gold wedding ring on your finger. Would you mind if I took a look at it?'

'Huh? Why?' Bulloch hesitated, but saw that both lawmen had their hands hovering persuasively over the butts of their guns. 'That an official request? Sure, here you are.'

Garrett peered inside the ring and read, 'To William from Mary.'

'Yeah, she's my wife.'

'Really? You know, I noticed the corpse you dragged in had a white ring of unsunburned flesh on his wedding finger. Like he was missing his ring. And you, I see, don't have a pale mark on your finger. Ergo, thou liest, as the immortal bard says.'

'OK, you've got me. Sure, I took it. But that don't prove nothing.'

'Well, while I was in Santa Fe I called on this Mary lady who identified the photo of the dead man as being her husband, Marshal William Dunwoody. This ring is the one she gave him many years ago. She, of course, is now a grieving widow.'

'OK, I ain't the marshal,' Bulloch admitted. 'So what? I didn't kill him. I just took his clothes.'

'And tried to pass yourself off as him.'

'You told me you were a marshal, Will-yum,' Selina blurted out. 'You showed me his badge, said it gave you licence to kill me.'

'Why don't you butt out? And you, too, Sheriff,' Bulloch shouted angrily. 'Sure I had a little game with you. But you got the wrong pig by the tail. I ain't breaking no laws. You're outa your jurisdiction.'

'Am I?' Garrett winked at the little gunshop owner who had craned forward to listen. 'Finding this interesting, pal? Well, listen on. Maybe you can tell me, *Will-yum*, or whoever you are, how you know so much about the case of Cotton Bulloch?'

The Texan shrugged. 'I read it in the news spreads. It was all over them, how some bitch sucked up to that guy, promised to marry him and all the time she was two-timing him with his best pal. If it happened to you, wouldn't you feel like giving them a lesson.'

'What, like killing the man that poor gal was really in love with, and kidnapping her, torturing and raping her, and finally killing her? She hadn't two-timed you, Bulloch, you just wouldn't leave her alone. I understand she was a pretty girl but not a pretty sight after you'd done with her.'

'Serve the bitch right,' Bulloch growled, going for his Remington. But the sheriff and his deputy were too fast for him, covering him with their guns before he had his halfway out of the holster.

'Cotton Bulloch, you're under arrest.' Garrett

grinned with triumph. 'There's a thousand-dollar reward out on you and you ain't gonna be getting no half-share.'

Jake Blackman, Poker Tom and Animal, trailed by Trick, Newt, and the surly older man, Pliny, jogged on their mustangs into the crowded bustle of White Oaks, turning up a side street that led to Selina's room above the stables.

'That's where that crazy dude's been staying, up there with the gal,' Poker Tom drawled. 'He's the only one I can think of who's been acting funny.'

'Yuh,' Animal agreed. 'Dat guy's real cuckoo.'

'Right, we'll take a look.'

'Duh, ain't we gonna see the parade?' Animal called, as Jake and Tom climbed the outside steps. 'I wanna have fun.'

Jake kicked in the locked door and the two men poked around inside the loft. It was not long before Jake found Mick's missing saddle-bags under the bed, packed with wads of forged greenbacks.

'Got him!' He slung the pack over his shoulder and stormed out. 'We'll be having fun all right,' he roared. 'With that funkin' Texan, when we find him.'

'He'll be in the Longhorn,' Tom said.

They left their horses and pushed their way across the crowded, noisy main street, bursting into the saloon.

Jake, his looks as black as his beard, spotted Bulloch instantly, and drew from under his coat his shoulder-hung Buntline Special with its fearsome sixteen-inch barrel. He'd paid a dollar for every extra inch. Now he intended to put it to good use. 'Right, you thieving jackanapes,' he hollered. 'Ye've been poking into my mine, ain't you?'

Sheriff Garrett spun on his spurred heel to meet him, his massive Magnum 357 still in his grip. 'What?'

'Not you.' Jake was almost frothing at the mouth with anger, uncaring that he was divulging secrets. 'That evil weevil! Him.'

'Yuh,' Animal agreed. 'We don't like wiggly weevils in duh biscuits. We gonna eradicate him. Cut off his bollocks and put 'em in de stew. Dat's what we gonna do.'

'This man's my prisoner and I'm taking him in,' Garrett warned. 'Put those guns away, boys.'

Jake brandished the saddle-bag and raged, 'This cash was in his room, stolen from me.'

Cotton Bulloch laughed contemptuously. 'It's all forged cash, you half-wits. I was bringing it in to show the sheriff. These are the ones you should be arresting, Garrett. I flushed 'em out. While you're frolicking with the governor in Santa Fe I've been doing the Feds job for 'em.'

Now even the lanky lawman was flustered. He knew his first duty was to protect his prisoner. But how? This mob meant business. So he tried placating them. 'Throw that forged cash down, Jake. This creep's for the high jump I can assure you. He's in my custody. I may have some questions for you later, but right now you can split the breeze.'

'What?' Jake screamed. 'That man hanged my mate, Mick. Hanged him, I say, in cold blood. He's gotta pay.'

'He will pay. He'll be hanged, too. There's no way he's getting off,' Garrett vowed. 'Right, I'm losing patience with you morons. Either disperse now, or we'll be putting you all in the calaboose.'

'Aw, no,' Animal slurred. 'We come here to have fun and dat's what we're gonna do.'

'Don't start something you'll regret,' Garrett snapped. 'I've had enough. I'm taking all you men into custody. Drop your guns.'

'No way,' Cotton jeered. 'I ain't sharing a stinkin' cell with them.'

All this time Jake had his right arm outstretched, the Buntline pointed unwavering at Bulloch, his finger on the trigger, his eyes gleaming, mercileesly.

*KA-room!* Lead, smoke and fire erupted from the long barrel. But, a split second before it did so, Bulloch, who had yet to be manacled, grabbed Garrett's arm, dodged down behind him and backed through the doorway to the bar. The bullet whistled past where he would have been, smashing woodwork, shelves, bottles and glasses. Harry Hawke ducked down, too, as bedlam ensued.

Garrett faced the onslaught, his Magnum bellowing, its large, blunt-nosed slug churning a hole through Jake's chest to hit the wall behind him.

Blackman went with it, collapsing in a bloody heap. His last word was, 'Shee-it!'

Selina rejoiced to see it. 'Thank you, Sheriff,' she screamed. 'Justice is done.'

'Get down!' Garrett shouted, placing his free hand on her head. He forced her down beneath a table and knelt beside her. 'Watch out, Hank!'

The warning came too late. Newt, incensed by the death of Jake, levered his Winchester carbine and its bullet smashed into Hank's side, knocking him, too, to the ground.

The others were fanning out, yelling and blazing away with their guns, as girls screamed and punters scrambled out of the way of the flying lead. All, that was, except Azariah Wilde, who coolly sat at his side table with his gun display before him and watched proceedings, carefully choosing Sam Colt's first self-cocker, a Lightning, with one of the first swing-out cylinders, brought out the year before, in '81.

'Get him!' Animal shouted, stumbling through chairs and tables to get a bead with his Thunderer on Garrett. And it looked as if he well might, for the sheriff had spent his six and was desperately trying to reload. 'Got you!' Animal gloated, aiming from pointblank range. 'You're a dead man, mister.'

'Not today,' Wilde remarked, neatly putting a .38 slug from the Lightning into Animal's back.

'Duh?' Animal shook his head, puzzled, but stayed standing. Wilde pumped in three more to bring the great hairy beast crashing down. 'I'm dead,' Animal groaned, as he lay on the floor.

Azariah Wilde turned his attentions to Poker Tom, who was spectacularly blazing away with both of his ivory-handled, twin .44s. Wilde's first shot rebounded off Tom's shiny leather chaps. 'Ouch!' he cried, hopping about in pain, trying to realign his Smith & Wessons.

'Stay still!' Wilde ordered in the silence during a break in the shooting. Tom gaped at him and did so. The gun merchant put his second shot impeccably between Tom's eyes, spinning him into an early grave. 'You won't be playing any more poker today,' Wilde muttered, primly.

But with murderous bloodlust, Newt was levering the Winchester's trigger guard, pumping out .52s, showering the cowering Selina and Garrett with glass and dust, splintering the table above their heads.

The sheriff succeeded in reloading amid the mayhem and din. He peered through the drifting carbide smoke and broken tables, carefully sighted the Magnum, squinting through one eye, and sent Newt catapulting back to smash into the wall.

Trick stared with amazement as his glassy-eyed pal slid to the floor. His own six-gun smoking and empty, he began to raise his hands.

Azariah Wilde had chosen a stub-nosed Cloverleaf house pistol from his array on the table. The first of his four bullets took Trick out. 'A great improvement,' he said, admiring the weapon, 'on the derringer.'

All his comrades gone, Pliny turned tail and charged towards the doorway. Garrett calmly shot him in the back. The blunt-nosed bullet propelled Pliny stumbling forward, desperately clawing for the batwings and freedom, leaving a trail of blood before he collapsed.

'Looks like they all gawn to the Great Unknown,' Cotton drawled, as he came up from behind the bar with Harry's single-barrel shotgun in his hands. 'Hallelujah!' He smashed it across the back of Garrett's head, felling him, then swung it on little Azariah, blasting him out of his chair.

'Come on,' he screamed at Selina. He tossed the weapon away and snatched up the sheriff's Magnum and the saddle-bags of forgeries, which he slung over his shoulder. Selina made no move, so he grabbed a hunk of her abundant hair and dragged her after him. 'You're coming with me, bitch.'

A military band was pumping out, 'America . . . America' as they emerged from the Longhorn.

In fact there was so much din going on nobody had noticed the fracas in the Longhorn, or, if they had, assumed it was part of the celebrations.

And now there was more bedlam in the street as 150 black troopers of the cavalry, led by the pompous Captain Henry Carroll, in his plumed helmet and dress uniform arrayed with a dazzling display of gilt braid and medals, his grey mount high-stepping, came under attack by racist, redneck miners.

They hurled flour-bag bombs and fireworks,

making the cavalrymen fight to retain their seats on their rearing and plunging terrified steeds.

Amid the cheers and screams other miners tried to demolish the flag-bedecked podium on which a bunch of terrified council bigwigs stood in readiness to take the salute.

Cotton held Selina by her wrist and steered her through the disarray as the podium wobbled and came toppling down. He had spied two horses hitched in an alleyway that looked as if they could run. 'Get on,' he roared, more or less tossing her into the saddle. He hauled himself on to the other and, leading Selina by her reins as she hung to the saddle horn, galloped out of White Oaks.

# TWELVE

Vince had headed his mustang away from the main trail and had followed Carrizo Creek. The horse's hoofs splashed through the shallow water as he urged it on and up through a twisting ravine, aiming to get behind the summit of El Capitan, perhaps to find refuge further north in the adobe village of Las Tablas. But he was unsure of how far he could go. The stabbing pain in his side made him gasp and fall forward, hanging around the mustang's neck as it carried him on wildly down another creek. Yes, this was the way, he was sure. But his head was spinning, and his eyes were seemingly unable to focus. . . .

Back at the stagecoach driver and guard had hefted the strongbox back on board and were checking the contents. 'There's only a couple of pokes missing,' the driver growled. 'It ain't too bad.'

Mrs Elsie Sullivan, whose husband ran the White Oaks dry-goods store, stuck her head out of the coach window again. 'That boy's gen'rally so polite when he comes into the store,' she screeched. 'Fancy talking to me like that. And pulling a gun on you.'

The shotgun asked, 'You mean you recognized him?'

'Oh, yes, that bandanna didn't fool me. It was the lad from Blazers Mills. I'd know his voice anywhere.'

'A curly-haired kid?' When she agreed, he muttered, 'You know, I had a feeling I'd met him before.'

'You mean that young sonuvagun who was in Henderson's beerhouse the other night?' the driver asked. 'Struck me then he had a desperate look.'

'When a kid like that's in trouble you never know what he'll do,' the shotgun agreed. 'He musta overheard us. I could have sworn he was asleep until Henderson kicked us out.'

'Just think,' the driver laughed. 'You treated him to a shot of your whiskey.'

'Waal, he's for the high jump now. Armed highway robbery's a hanging offence.'

'With that bullet in him,' the driver muttered, 'I doubt if he'll last through the night.'

'What are you going to do?' Mrs Sullivan demanded. 'I'll be late for my sister's funeral.'

'Ain't much we can do but head on,' the guard replied. 'We'll cable the White Oaks office from Lincoln. They'll soon have his description out all over the territory. He won't get far.'

Benny Brunelli was busy loading up his wagon,

preparing to leave, as Abigail Blackman and her brood of brats watched. 'Ain't you going back to the mine to collect that equipment of your'n?' she asked.

'No, I ain't. You can keep that. I can soon get some more when I get started again. *If* I do. I'm thinking of taking up a more honest profession when I reach the coast. All this has been a bit of a strain. I'll never forget Mick's face. That might have been me hanging there.'

'You worry too much, Benny. A pity we can't all come along. It'd be nice to have a change of scene.'

'I couldn't do that to my best pal Jake. Run off with his wife?' Benny glanced at the noisy rabble of kids. 'No way. I'm an honourable man.'

Just then, however, a mustang came clopping into the yard, his reins hanging free, a youth slumped forward in the saddle. There was a sticky patch of blood on his shirt.

One of the boys caught hold of the reins to bring him to a halt and Vince slid from the saddle, hitting the ground hard. He lay there, breathing hard, looking up at the faces that seemed to be wavering over him.

'He's been shot,' Benny said, jumping down from the wagon to kneel beside him. 'What you been up to, pal?'

'Robbed the stage,' Vince whispered through his dry lips.

'That was a damn fool thing to do. You got the posse after you?'

'No, don't think so.' Vince gritted his teeth against the pain and gasped, 'I'm bleeding bad.'

Abigail bent down, pulled up Vince's shirt and took a look. She poked at the bloody hole with a filthy finger. 'Looks to me like the slug musta bounced offen his ribs and gone right on through. In that case you maybe got a chance, buster. Turn him over, Benny. Let's see what it's like on t'other side.'

She wiped her nose with her finger and croaked to the oldest boy, 'Elmer, go git me a bit of kitchen rag. Wet it in the bucket first.'

Vince cried out with pain as they hauled him over. 'Hm,' Benny mused, eyeing the wound. 'Not too good. Let's help him up and lay him in the shade. It's too hot here.' Flies were homing in on the bloody hole halfway down the side of the youth's bronzed back.

When they had settled him on the built-up wooden veranda outside the cabin door, Abigail took the wet rag and tried to plug the hole. 'Go git me another for t'other side.'

'Ain't you got a sheet?' Benny asked. 'We need to bandage him up.'

'Sheets? What are they? Elmer,' she hollered, 'bring one of Daddy's shirts.'

When they had tied the wadding tight Vince lay back and murmured, 'I don't feel good. You think I'm going to die?'

'There's a distinct possibility of that; what you might call the natural result of such dangerous pur-

142

suits,' Benny remarked. 'But one thing, sonny, you got youth, health and strength on your side. Maybe you got a chance.'

'Maybe if I could rest up here a bit? I thought I could head on north to the Cienaga del Macho,' Vince gasped out, after Benny had fed him a mug of water. 'Maybe I can . . . thanks, mister.'

'He's passed out,' Benny called, as Vince lay back and closed his eyes. 'He's still breathing, but for how long?'

'Maybe we should go git the sawbones,' Abigail mused. 'Seems a shame for a nice-looking kid like him to cop, it.'

'Lady, I ain't ridin' into White Oaks to fetch no doctor,' Benny sang out. 'My own position here is somewhat perilous. In fact, it's high time I was moving on.'

'Hey, look at this, Ma,' Elmer shouted, brandishing two-handed the heavy Navy Colt revolver he had found in the haversack hanging from the mustang's saddle horn.

'You bring that over here,' his mother screamed. 'Take your finger of the funkin' hammer!'

When he did so she laid it on the boards on the other side of Vince and emptied the haversack. 'Waal, lookee here.' She poured gold dust from one of the pouches into her palm. 'The real McCoy.'

'Wow!' Benny snatched up the other pouch. 'Bagsie this one. You keep that one, sweetheart. Looks like you'll be buryin' him, anyhow.'

He started back towards the wagon. 'I gotta be on my way. So long, y'all. Give my regards to Jake.'

As he was trying to climb back on the box, with some difficulty due to his short legs, a stranger and a pretty girl came riding their horses into the yard.

'Hold it right there, short-arse,' Cotton Bulloch growled, waving the Magnum at Benny. 'Hand over your piece.'

'I don't carry one,' Benny replied. 'They have a nasty habit of going off.'

Bulloch nudged his mustang over and reached out, sticking the Magnum under Benny's nose and frisking his pockets. 'What do we have here?' He grinned, whisking out the pouch of dust. 'Just what I need. I'm heading north.'

'Not another,' Benny sighed. 'That's Wells Fargo property, mister. You'll have to explain the situation to *them.*'

'Who the hell are *you*? Hang on, I've seen you along at the mine. You're the forger.'

'You . . .' Benny gulped. 'You . . . Mick?'

'Mick? Oh, yeah. God rest his soul. So where you think you're off to, duck's disease?'

'Me? Nowhere special.'

'You sure ain't. Jump down on those little legs of yourn.'

'There's no need to be rude,' Benny said, as he clambered to the ground.

'Who else is around?' Bulloch demanded, turning the Magnum towards the cabin and glancing at the barn and sheds.

'Nobody,' Abigail yelled. 'Jake an' the boys have gone to town. Won't be back fer a few days. Ain't that so, kids?'

Elmer piped up. 'We're here on our own. But I wouldn't try anythang, mister. My ma's got a shotgun.'

'Has she? That's mighty interesting. You better go and fetch it, sonny. And make sure to unload it, if you know how.'

'He knows,' Abigail said. 'Do what the man says, Elmer. Don't you try nuthin' or this ornery bastard'll kill you.'

'I might even do that.' Bulloch gave his creepy smile that struck a chill down Selina's spine. 'So git!'

When the ten-year-old boy returned he pointed the twelve-guage at Bulloch with a sullen look and for moments they thought he was going to try his luck. Then he meekly handed it over. Bulloch grinned, smashed it on a nearby anvil and tossed it away. 'Now I'm the only one with a gun.'

Slumped in the shadows, where he had been lying unnoticed, Vince suddenly stirred and groaned.

'Who the hell's that?'

'Just some kid,' Benny said. 'Don't worry, he's as good as dead, got shot trying to rob the stage. That's who I got the gold dust from. That's all he had.'

Selina darted forward as Cotton Bulloch aimed the Magnum at the figure lying on the porch. She fell over him to protect him, running her fingers through his sweat-damp hair. 'Vince, you fool. You awful fool. Why?'

'Is that you, Selina?' Vince tried to raise his head. 'I did it for you.'

The girl's eyes filled with tears as she saw the bloody shirt tied tight around his chest. 'It's all right,' she called back to Bulloch. 'Don't shoot! It's Vincent . . . my friend.'

Then she spotted the long-barrelled Navy Colt lying on the far side of Vince and quickly put an arm across to push it underneath the youth's back. 'We need to get him to the infirmary at the fort. He's in a bad way.'

'What?' Bulloch strode across. 'Oh, it's him, your *dangerous* friend.' He broke into sardonic laughter, poking Vince with the Magnum. 'Look at the sap. You ever seen such a washout? Robbed the stage and got himself shot. What was he trying to do, impress you?'

Selina met his eyes. 'Yes, he probably was. I've told you! I must get him to the fort. I can't leave him here to die.'

'Shut up.' The Texan back-handed her hard across the face. 'Ain't you got the message yet? You're my gal. We're getting outa here. Headin' north, Colorado, Montana, maybe on to Oregon. We'll spread this fake moolah around as we go. Nobody's gonna catch up with us.'

Vince raised himself on one elbow. 'Leave her alone.'

146

Bulloch smashed his fist into Vince's jaw. 'There,' he growled, as Vince fell back. 'That should finish him. Say goodnight to your li'l darlin'.'

The Texan was wondering how many bullets he had left. He couldn't afford to waste any. That was why he hadn't shot the youth. Well, *he* wouldn't last long. But what about these others?

'I got news for you,' he shouted at the woman. 'Jake won't be coming back. Not tomorrow. Not ever. Him and his clowns are all dead.'

'No!' Abigail shrilled her grief, but it was mostly for herself. 'What will happen to us? How can we survive? You murderer—'

'*I* didn't kill 'em. I was under arrest.' Cotton laughed at her exaggerated grief. 'Garrett and some li'l gunrunner squirt did. Made a good job of it. Like cleaning out a nest of rats. Why the squirt poked his nose in I don't know. But it was the last thing he did. I shoulda finished the sheriff but I was in a bit of a hurry to get out.'

'That was a mistake.' Benny shook his head dolefully. 'Garrett ain't one to give up. He'll be coming after you.'

Bulloch had dragged the girl away from Vince with an iron grip around her wrist. 'I'll be ready for him. Anyway, we're gonna show him our dust.'

'Please, Will-yum,' Selina pleaded. 'You go on your own. You don't need me no more. I'll take Vince to the fort. I won't tell them where you are.'

'Are you mad?' Bulloch screamed, not realizing

147

that he was the one who was mad. 'Nobody gives witness against *me*. Nobody points the sheriff and his posse on their way. Get ready to leave. I gotta dispose of this lot.'

Selina could hardly believe her ears. Or eyes. He was jabbing the big revolver at Abigail and the three older children, ordering, 'Come on, up against the wall.'

The children started wailing, clinging to their mother as if they sensed what he was going to do. 'You, too,' he sang out to Benny. 'Come and join us.'

'You *wouldn't*?' Benny reluctantly approached. 'Not the kids?'

'Mister, I couldn't give a damn. Man, woman, child.' The Texan had a manic look in his eyes and was licking spittle from his lips as if excited. He holstered the Magnum, and pulled a long, razor-sharp Bowie from his belt scabbard. 'Ever butchered hogs, pal? Waal, put yourself in their place. But try not to squeal.'

'No,' Abigail wailed, hoisting her skirts and pulling out the pouch of gold dust. 'Take this. It's all we got. Spare us.'

'Thanks. You wanna go first or last? Come on, pal. Over here. What you hanging about for?'

'No!' Selina screamed out and snatched the Magnum .357 out of Bulloch's holster. She backed away, pointing the heavy gun at him. 'I won't let you.'

'What?' Bulloch grinned at her, holding out his hand. 'You ain't got the nerve to kill me. You said so yourself. Hand it over.'

'No!' As he took a step towards Selina she tossed the gun over his head to Benny. 'Kill him,' she screamed.

'What?' Benny caught the Magnum and fumbled with it, trying to point it at Bulloch and pull the trigger, not realizing that the safety catch was on. 'How?'

'You half-wit!' Bulloch strode towards him, knife at the ready, dragging Selina with him. 'Give me that.'

'Bulloch!' Vince had struggled upright, gasping with effort. He swung his legs off the veranda and gripped the Navy Colt in his hands, trying to focus on the man. 'You filthy murdering coward.'

'What?' Bulloch spun on his heel. 'You!' He tried to drag Selina before him as a shield, putting the knife to her neck. As the Navy barked out he simultaneously stuck the Bowie into her throat, hard, slitting the white flesh apart. As blood seeped out the bullet struck him like a sledgehammer blow, knocking him off his feet to lie flat on his back in the dust.

'No,' he pleaded, as Vince staggered towards him. He tried to crawl away. 'I didn't mean to . . . I wasn't going to. . . .' Vince pumped shots into him as he approached, into his head, his leg, his shoulder, and finally, when he was right over him, into his heart. 'You black-hearted bastard,' he sobbed out.

His knees gave way and he slumped down on to the girl. 'Selina, no, don't leave me,' he begged, as he reached out to grip her hand. 'Please.'

But the blood was spurting from her; her life was ebbing away. She gripped hold of his fingers and gasped out, 'Vince . . . forgive me.'

'The Song of the Whip' the Mexicans called it. The plaited rawhide sang through the air cutting the cloth of the youth's white cotton shirt, dyeing it crimson with blood as a crowd of them watched, their dark faces impassive. In days not long before when this land was part of the old Spanish colonial empire such whippings would have been commonplace.

Vince almost screamed at the first cut, but bit hard on the piece of wood between his teeth, fixed there to stop him biting off his tongue. Again the bullwhips flashed like striking snakes and again he longed to cry out, to beg for mercy. But he braced himself. It was the punishment he had chosen. He had to endure it. He was suspended by his wrists to Lincoln town's whipping-post as his back was flayed as if by fire and the two deputies laid on, alternately, counting the strokes to fifty. Only fifty more to go.

As the lash hissed through the air Vince groaned and his mind spun with memories of how after the shooting he had lain for two weeks semi-conscious in the infirmary at Fort Stanton uncaring whether he lived or died. But one day he had awoken and the sun was shining and he knew he wanted to live.

After that there had been the four months in the dark, dank cellar, beneath the Lincoln courthouse, the only accommodation for prisoners. Alone with the forger, Benny – apart from the occasional drunk or horse-thief – he awaited the twice-yearly visit of the circuit judge.

Like Billy Bonney before them, at first they were only allowed out under guard to visit the privy at the back. Pat Garrett had instructed his new deputies to take no chances. Two such men had died when The Kid had grabbed a gun and blasted them both to smithereens.

Gradually Garrett realized, however, that these two were no psychopaths like Billy, and he gave them some leeway, allowing them out in chains to do community service, cleaning up Lincoln's middens and the piles of rubbish left in the streets to be buried in deep trenches. Sometimes the sheriff would sit with them in the shade of a pine and watch the sparkling Hondo and time flowing fast as the tubby little Benny cheerfully joshed and swapped yarns with Garrett. Indeed, towards the end he occasionally allowed them to come up of an evening to join him on the veranda overlooking the town square and relish the coolness of the night. Not that he ever passed the bottle across. He drew the line at that.

One evening the little gunshop man, Azariah Wilde, in his derby and neat suit, was there. 'I really thought you were dead,' Garrett hooted, recalling the bloodbath at White Oaks.

'Hardly.' Wilde gave a glimmer of a grin, and explained for their benefit, 'I was testing a newfangled body armour under my shirt, kinda like the chain mail those knights of old used to wear. The force of the blast knocked me off my chair, but I was otherwise unharmed. A successful experiment one might say. Found lead pellets in the vest afterwards.'

The prisoners were not to know that Wilde was another secret service agent, sent by Washington to find out what was going on in Lincoln. 'I had an idea events were gonna get explosive that day,' he said. He got to his feet. 'I guess I'll be shutting up shop and heading back to Santa Fe.'

But that was long before the judge eventually arrived. When he did get there Garrett took supper with him privately and said, 'Seems to me, sir, like this kid was enamoured of the dancin' gal. You know what you're like at that age. He tried robbing the stage to get some cash to rescue her from her life of sin. I might point out nobody got hurt, apart from himself, the gold was recovered, he took out a notorious criminal, and it's his first offence. If you're inclined to be lenient I've an idea it will be his last. You send him to territorial prison he could well turn bad. It could be the end for him.'

'There's got to be some deterrent,' the judge replied. 'Armed robbery of the mail generally earns five years.'

'You've pleaded guilty so you can take your choice,' Garrett reported to Vince. 'A long term inside or a public flogging.'

'I can't stand being cooped up. I want to be free,'

Vince replied. 'I'll take the whipping.'

Abigail had arrived on her wagon to visit Benny. 'I'm runnin' the ranch better than that lazy lickspittle Jake ever did,' she told him. The boys, aged ten and eleven years, were nearly full-grown and able to pull their weight. 'I brought ya a special treat,' she cooed, handing him a pail of her soup.

'*Hay-zoos*!' Benny cried, as he took a tentative sniff. 'It's a wonder that sonuvabitch Jake survived as long as he did.'

The next morning Benny was taken up first and returned to announce, 'Five years in the slammer. It ain't too bad. Abigail says she'll wait for me. Then maybe we'll go to California. Maybe we won't.'

As Vince was taken up Benny called, 'Good luck, son.'

Since the arrival of sharp lawyers in New Mexico flogging had fallen out of favour. But the judge had decided to revive it.

'The sheriff reckons you've got the grit to change your ways, stay out of trouble and lead a decent life. He figures you're the kind of young fellow this territory needs to pull it out of the dark ages. So,' the judge lectured, 'Take this chance.'

The sentence of one hundred lashes came as a shock. Vince had expected twenty at most. Now as he hung from the post the flogging seemed interminable. The Song of the Whip whistled across his back, cutting the flesh to ribbons. Vince was barely conscious as they cut him down and dragged him back to the empty cellar. Garrett told a Mexican woman to rub tecole ointment – usually used to keep the worms at bay when heifers had their ears bobbed – into the whip wounds. Gradually Vince's jangled nerves settled. The next day he managed to get to his feet to be taken up to the sheriff's office.

'Release his chains,' Garrett ordered, for Vince was still bound ankles to wrists. 'You're free to go.' He took the long-barrelled Navy Colt and a few dollars from his drawer. 'Sign for the return of your property. Take it.'

'Is that it?'

'What more you want.' Garrett gave his toothy horse grin as Vince turned to leave. 'Aw, hang on. I was planning on this being mine. But it seems you're the one who shot down that cold-blooded killer, so it's yourn.'

'What?'

'What you think? The thousand-dollar reward from Fort Worth. See, your name's on the cheque, you lucky sonuvagun. You just hand this over at the bank and they'll cough up the cash. And don't go spending it all on wild wimmin and whiskey.'

'No,' Vince muttered, 'I won't.'

It was November by now and a bitter down-draught was blowing from the mountains presaging the winter to come. Vince cashed a hundred of the money and opened a bank account for himself. He bought a warm wool shirt, fur-lined jacket, a flat-topped Stetson and 'a stout leather belt to stuff the revolver into. In the window of Dolan's store he saw that Dowlin's Mill on the Rio Ruidoso was up for sale at an asking price of $1,000. It gave him an idea and, for the first time feeling more like a man than a boy, he rode out of Lincoln on a ten-dollar horse, and headed south to the fast-flowing Ruidoso. The sawmill was a bit ramshackle and the widower, Dan Dowlin, was keen to leave the territory, so agreed a price of $850, 'lock, stock and barrel', as he said.

It had started to snow as Vince rode on up into the high country and cut twenty miles across to the Rio Tularosa to Blazer's Mills. Doc was in the sawyard as he rode in.

'You OK?' Joseph Blazer asked.

'Sure, I'm fine.'

'I can't give you your job back. I've taken on a new man.'

Vince grinned and explained the situation. 'I'm gonna be in competition now.'

'You make sure you take your time seasoning the wood like I told you. Folks are in too much of a damn hurry these days.'

'Yes, sir, you've taught me good.'

'You come for your mustang?'

Vince nodded. 'And Selina.'

'She's working in the agency store. She healed good, but that drunken surgeon made a mess of the' stitches. I guess it *was* the Fourth of July. Still, Abigail and Benny saved both your lives, I understand, before Garrett reached the scene.'

'I'll go see her.'

'Vince,' Doc Blazer called out. 'Prepare yourself for a bit of a shock. She ain't the pretty gal she was.'

Not sure what Doc meant, Vince found Selina in the store as two Mescalero squaws bartered with her for extra blankets. When she saw him she recoiled like a wild animal in its lair, looking around desperately, her hand going to the vivid white scars on her throat and jaw. Cotton Bulloch's knife had cut deep, miraculously missing the jugular by a fraction. But it had done bad damage, leaving her with her mouth slightly skewed, affecting her speech which came out in a slur. 'No!' she cried, backing away behind the squaws as Vince approached. 'Don't look at me.'

She covered her face with her hands, hiding beneath her mass of black curls, whispering, 'Go away. It's God's punishment. I'm no good, Vince. You don't want me.'

He gently parted her hands and cupped her sweet face in his. 'I'll always want you, Selina. I knew that from the first moment I saw you. I always will. You know that. I'm scarred, too. We're different. But inside we're the same. That's what counts.'

Selina clung to him. 'Oh, Vince,' she cried. 'Really, after all I done to you?' But then their words were lost as they hugged each other close, kissing and caressing, and the squaws clapped and laughed.

They rode out of the mill, Selina sitting sidesaddle behind him, on his mustang, clinging to his waist and

156

wrapped in her warm winter coat. On the way who should they meet but the Mexican family who had given him shelter the night before he robbed the stage. They were bringing their flock down to the lower pastures for the winter and to live in their *jacal* at the village of San Patricio.

'*Hola!*' the herder called, but his daughter's face fell as she saw Selina. She was carrying a lamb in her arms and could not hide her disappointment. But she bravely smiled when she heard their news.

'We are going to be wed.' Vince turned to meet Selina's snow-veiled blue eyes. 'I've bought the mill. We'll hold a big party. You must all come.'

They rode on down the Ruidoso to their new home, the sound of the *peon* woman's blessing ringing out in the cold air.

'*Vaya con Dios,*' and the daughter singing out that she wished that they might have many children and a '*hermoso hijo.*'

'She hopes we will have a handsome son,' he said.

Selina squeezed herself into him. 'We will,' she sighed. 'We will.'

# AUTHOR'S AFTERWORD

In the Washington National Archives are the daily reports of US secret service agent Azariah Wilde. He refers not only to his assistance to Sheriff Pat Garrett in putting paid to the Billy Bonney gang in 1881 but also to his undercover surveillance at White Oaks of Dan Deidricks livery stable. He believed it to be the hub of forgers who were flooding New Mexico with many thousands of dollars in counterfeit bills. His main suspects were Poker Tom Emory and Animal Bousman.

With no more information available I began to imagine what Wilde was like and what might have happened. Therefore, although real-life men like Garrett, Wilde, Ash Upson, Governor Wallace and Doc Blazer populate this resulting story the main events and other characters are entirely fictional.

J.D.